A MAN OBSESSED

A MAN OBSESSED

by Alan E. Nourse

TABLE OF CONTENTS

CHAPTER ONE

Jeffrey Meyer sat back in his chair and waited. He could hardly breathe in the stifling air of the place. His hand clenched his glass until the knuckles were white, and his lip curled slightly as he watched the crowd around him. His whole body was tense. His legs, knotted tightly under the seat, were ready to move in an instant, and his eyes roved from the front to the back of the place. They were pale gray eyes that were never still—moving, watching, waiting. He had waited for so long, waited and hunted with bitter patience. But now he knew the long wait was drawing to a close. He knew that Conroe was coming and the trap was set.

For the thousandth time that evening, a shiver of chilly pleasure passed through him at the thought. He squirmed in eagerness, hardly daring to breathe. With his free hand he caressed the cool plastic handle of the gun that was close to his side, and a tight smile appeared on his thin lips. Conroe was coming ... at last ... at last.... And tonight he would kill Conroe.

The place was a madhouse around him. In the front of the room, by the street door, was a long horseshoe bar. It was already crowded by the early revelers. A screechie in the corner blatted out the tinny, nervous music that had recently become so popular, and a loud, hysterical burst of feminine laughter echoed to the back of the room.

Jeff Meyer rubbed his eyes, smarting from the bluish haze filling the long, low-ceilinged room. The unhealthy laughter broke out again, and someone burst into a bellow of song, half giggle, half noise.

At the adjoining table an alky-siky stirred, muttered something unintelligible and returned his nose sadly to his glass. Jeff's eyes flicked over the man with distaste. The scrawny neck, the sagging jaw, the idiotic, almost unearthly expression of intent listening on the vapid face: a typical picture of the type. Jeff watched him for a moment in disgust, then moved his eyes on, still watching as a flicker of apprehension passed through his mind.

A girl, quite naked except for the tray slung at her waist, strolled by his table, wagging her hips and turning on her heaviest personality smile.

"Drive a nail, mister?"

"Beat it."

The smile cooled slightly on the girl's lips. "Just askin'," she whined. "You don't have to get—"

"Beat it!" Jeff shot her a venomous look, trying frantically to keep his attention from straying from the front of the room. It would be too much to slip up now, more than he could stand to make a mistake like the last time.

The trap was perfect. It *couldn't* fail this time. Each step of the way had been carefully sketched, plotted through long sleepless nights of conference and planning. They couldn't have hunted a man like Conroe all these years without learning something about him—about his personality, about the things he liked and disliked, the things he did, the places he frequented, the friends he made.

Last time, after Jeff's own blundering error had allowed him to slip through the net at the last frantic minute, there seemed to be no hope. Everything seemed all the more hopeless when the man had disappeared as completely as if he were dead. But then they had found the girl—the key to his hiding place. She had formed the top link in the long, meticulous chain which had been drawn tighter each day, drawing Paul Conroe at last closer and closer to the hands of the man who was going to kill him. And now the trap was set; there could be no slip this time. There might never be another chance.

The street door opened sharply, and a short, bull-necked man with sandy hair walked in. He was followed by two other men in neat business suits. The first man stepped quickly to the bar, shouldering his way through the crowd, and stood sipping beer for several minutes. He glanced closely at the people around the bar and the surrounding tables before he walked toward the back and seated himself next to Meyer. Looking at Jeff with an indefinable expression, he finished his beer at a gulp and set the glass down on the table top with a snap.

"What's up?" Jeff said hoarsely.

"Something's funny." The sandy-haired man's voice was a smooth bass, and a frown appeared on his pink forehead. "He should have been here by now. He left the hotel over in Camden-town an hour ago, private three-wheeler, and he headed for here."

6

Jeff leaned forward, his face going white. "You've got somebody on him?"

"Yes, yes, of course." The man's voice was sharp, and there were tired lines around his eyes. "Take it easy, Jeff. You wouldn't be able to get him if he did come in—the way you are. He'd spot you in two seconds."

Jeff's hand trembled as he gripped his glass, and he settled tensely back in his chair. "It can't go wrong, Ted. It's got to come off."

"It should. The girl is here and she got word from him last night."

"Can she be trusted?"

The sandy-haired man shrugged. "Don't be silly. In this game, nobody can be trusted. If she's scared enough, she'll play along—okay? We've done our best to scare her. We've scared the hell out of her. Maybe she's more scared of Conroe—I don't know. But it looks cold to me. On a platter. So get a grip on yourself."

"It's got to come off." Jeff growled the words savagely, and drained his glass at a gulp. The sandy-haired man blinked, his pale little eyes curious. He leaned back thoughtfully. "Suppose it doesn't, Jeff? Suppose something goes wrong? Then what?"

Jeff's heavy hand caught the man's wrist in a grip that was like a vise. "You don't talk like that," he grated. "Your men I don't mind, but not you—understand? It can't go wrong. That's all there is to it. No if's, no maybe's. You got that now?"

Ted rubbed his wrist, his face red. "All right," he muttered. "So it can't go wrong. So I shouldn't talk, I shouldn't ask questions. But if it does go wrong, you're going to be dead. Do you know that? Because you're killing yourself with this—" He sighed, staring at Meyer. "What's it worth, Jeff? This constant tearing yourself apart? You've been obsessed with it for years. I know, I've been working with you and watching you for the last five of them—five long years of hunting. And for what? To get a man and kill him. That's all. What's it worth?"

Jeff took a deep breath and took a pack of cigarettes from his jacket. "Drive a nail," he said, offering the pack. "And don't worry about me. Worry about Conroe. He's the one who'll be dead."

Ted shrugged and took the smoke. "Okay. But if this blows up, I'm through. Because this is all I can take."

"Nothing will blow up. I'll get him. If I don't get him now, I'll get him the next time, or the next, or the next. With or without you, I'll get him."

Jeff took a trembling breath, his gray eyes cold under heavy black brows. "But there hadn't better be any next time."

He sat back in his chair, his face falling into the lines so familiar to Ted Bahr. Jeff Meyer had been a handsome man, before the long years of hate had done their work on his face. He was a huge, powerfully built man, heavy-shouldered, with a strong neck and straight nose, and a shock of jet black hair, neatly clipped. Only his face showed the bitterness of the past five years—years filled with anger and hatred, and a growing savagery which had driven the man almost to the breaking point.

The lines about his eyes and mouth were cruel—heavy lines that had been carved deeply and indelibly into the strong face, giving it a harsh, almost brutal cast in the dim light of the bistro. He breathed regularly and slowly as he sat, but his pale eyes were ice-hard as they moved slowly across the little show floor. They took in every face, every movement in the growing throng.

He was out of place and he knew it. He had no use for the giddy, half-hysterical people who crowded these smoke-filled holes night after night. They came in droves from the heart of the city to drink the watery gin and puff frantically on the contraband cigarettes as they tried desperately to drive off the steam and pressure of their daily lives.

Meyer hated the smell and stuffiness of the place; he hated the loud screams of laughter, the idiotic giggles; he hated the blubbering alky-sikys who crowded the bars with their whisky and their strange, unearthly dream-worlds. Above all, he hated the horrible, resounding artificiality, the brassiness and clanging noise of the crowd. His skin crawled. He knew that he couldn't possibly disappear into such a crowd, that he was as obvious, sitting there, as if he had been painted with red polka dots. And he knew that if Conroe spotted him a second before he spotted Conroe—He eased back in the chair and fought for control of his trembling hands.

The lights dimmed suddenly and a huge red spotlight caught the curtain at the back of the show floor. Jeff heard Bahr catch his breath for a moment, then let out a small, uneasy sigh. The crowd hushed as the girl parted the curtains and stepped out onto the middle of the floor, to a fanfare of tinny music. Jeff's eyes widened as they followed her to the center of the red light.

"That's her."

Jeff glanced sharply at Bahr. "The girl? She's the one?"

Bahr nodded. "Conroe knows how to pick them. He's supposed to meet her later. This is her first show for the evening. Then she has another at ten and another at two. He's supposed to take her home." He glanced around the room carefully. "Watch yourself," he muttered, and silently slipped away from the table.

The girl was nervous. Jeff sat close enough to see the fear in her face as she whirled around the floor. The music had shifted into a slow throbbing undertone, as she started to dance. She moved slowly, circling the floor. Her hair was long and black, flowing around her shoulders, and her body moved with carefully calculated grace to the music. But there was fear in her face as she whirled, and her eyes sought the faces on the fringe of the circle.

The music quickened imperceptibly and Jeff felt a chill run up his spine. The upper part of the shimmering gown slipped from the girl's shoulders, and slowly the tempo of the dance began to change from the stately rhythm it had a moment before. The throb of the music became hypnotic, moving faster and faster. Jeff's hands trembled as he tried to draw his eyes away from the undulating figure. There had been nothing to mark the change, but suddenly the dance had become obscene as the music rose—so viciously obscene that Jeff nearly gagged.

He felt the tension in the crowd around him. He heard their breathing rise, felt the desperate eagerness in their hard, bright eyes as they watched. The nervousness had left the girl's face. She had forgotten her fear, and a little smile appeared on her face as her body moved in abandon to the quickening beat.

Slowly she moved toward the tables, and the spotlight followed her, playing tricks with her hair and gown, concealing and revealing, twisting and swaying.... Jeff felt his body freeze. He fought to move, fought to take his eyes from the writhing figure as she drew closer and closer—

And then she was among the people, moving from table to table, never slowing her motion, graceful as a cat, twisting and twirling in the flickering red light. In and out she moved until she reached Jeff's table, her face inscrutable—a peacefully smiling mask. With amazing grace she leaped up on the table top and gave Jeff's glass a kick that sent it spinning onto the floor with a crash. And then the red light hit him full in the face—

"Get out of the light!"

Like a cat he threw his chair back and struck the girl, knocking her from the table. Someone screamed and the light swung to the girl, then back to him. The table went over. He rolled out of the light, twisting and fighting through the stunned and screaming crowd. His gun was in his hand, and he frantically searched the shouting room with his eyes.

"Get him! There he goes!"

He heard Bahr's voice roar from the side of the room. Jeff swung sharply to the sound of the voice. He saw the tall, slender figure crouched with his back to the bar, eyes wide with fear and desperation. There was no mistaking the face, the hollow cheeks and the high forehead, the graying hair. It was the face he had seen in his dreams, the twisted lips, the evil, ghoulish face of the man he had hunted to the ends of the earth. For a fraction of a second he saw Paul Conroe, crouched at bay, and then the figure was gone, twisting through the crowd toward the door—

"Stop him!" Jeff swung savagely into the crowd, screaming at Bahr across the room. "He's heading for the street! Get him!" The gun kicked sharply against his hand as he fired at the moving head. Rising for an instant, it disappeared again into the sea of heads. A scream rose at the shot. Women dropped to the floor, glasses crashed, tables went over. Someone clawed ineffectually for Jeff's leg. Then, abruptly, the lights went out and there was another scream.

"The door, the door—Don't let him get out—"

Jeff plunged to the side of the room, wrenched open the emergency exit and plunged down the dark, narrow walkway to the street. He heard shots as he ran. Turning the corner of the building, he saw the tall figure running pell-mell down the wet street.

"There he goes! Get him!"

Ted Bahr hung from the door. He gasped as he held his side, his face twisted in pain. "He hit me," he panted. "He's broken away—" A jet car slid from the curb and whined down the street toward the fleeing figure. "He can't make it—I've got men on every corner in cars. They'll get him, drive him back—"

"But where's he going?" A sob of rage choked Jeff's voice. "She sold us out, the bitch. She fingered me when she saw him come in—" His whole body trembled and the words tumbled out, almost incoherent. "But he must know the streets are blocked. Where's he running?"

"You think I'm a mind reader? I don't know. There are no open buildings in the whole block but this place and the Hoffman Center. He can't go anywhere else and he can't get out of the block. We've got every escapeway sewed up tight. He'll have to come back here or be shot down out there."

They watched the gloomy street, tears of rage in Jeff's eyes. His hands shook uncontrollably and his shoulders sagged in exhaustion and defeat. The tavern door had burst open and people were crowding out. Jeff and Ted Bahr moved back into the shadows of the alleyway and waited and listened.

"There's got to be a shot!" Jeff burst out. "He couldn't have slipped through." He turned to Bahr frantically. "Could he have gone into the Center?"

"On what pretense? They'd throw him to the Mercy Men—or the booby hatch, one or the other. He'd know better than to try." The sandy-haired man sank down on his haunches and gripped his side tightly. "He'll be back or we'll hear the shooting. He couldn't have slipped through."

A three-wheeled jet car slid in to the curb, and a man came up to them, eyes wide. "Get him?"

Bahr scowled. "No sign. How about the other boys?"

The man blinked. "Not a whisper. He never reached the end of the block."

"Did you check with Klett and Barker?"

"They haven't seen a soul down here."

Bahr glanced at Jeff sharply. "How about the streets behind? Any chance of a breakthrough there?"

The man's voice was matter-of-fact. "It's airtight. He couldn't get through without somebody seeing him." He stepped back to the car and spoke rapidly into the talker for a moment or two. "Nothing yet."

"Damn. How about Howie and the boys inside the place?"

"Nothing from them either."

Jeff's face darkened. "The Hoffman Center," he said slowly. "He got into the Center, somehow. He must have."

"He'd have to have gilt-edged medical credentials to get in after hours. They don't mess around over there. And what would it gain him?"

Jeff peered at Bahr in the darkness. "Maybe he wanted to be thrown to the Mercy Men. Maybe he's figured that as a last resort, he'll go in and volunteer, make a stab at the Big Cash."

Bahr stared at the big man in horror. "Look—Conroe may be desperate, but he hasn't lost his mind. My God, man! He isn't crazy."

"But he's scared."

"Of course he's scared, but—"

"How scared?"

Bahr shrugged angrily. "He'd have to be on his last legs to take a gamble like that."

"But they'd take him. They wouldn't ask any questions. They'd swallow him up; *they'd hide him*, whether they knew it or not." Jeff's voice rose in excitement. "Look. We've hunted him down for years. We've never rested; we've never quit. He knows that and he knows why. He knows me. He knows I'm not going to quit until I get him. And he knows I will get him, sooner or later. I'm cutting too close; I'm undermining his friends; I'm always moving closer. Everywhere he goes, everything he does, I'm onto him. And he knows when I do get him, he's going to die. What does that add up to?"

Bahr blinked in silence. Jeff's face hardened. "Well, I'll tell you what it adds up to. A man can take just so much. He can slide and twist and hide and keep moving just so long. Then he finds there aren't any more hiding places. But there's one last place a man can go to hide—if he's really at the end of his tether—and that's the Mercy Men. Because there he could vanish as though he'd never existed."

Ted Bahr carefully lit a smoke. "If that's where he went, we're through, Jeff. We'll never get him. We don't even need to worry about trying. Because if he's gone there, he'll never come out again."

"Some of them do."

Bahr grunted. "One in a million, maybe. The odds are so heavy that there's no sense thinking about it. If Paul Conroe has gone to the Mercy Men, then he's dead. And that is that."

Jeff returned his weapon to his pocket sharply and walked out to the car at the curb. "Keep your men where they are," he said to Bahr. "Keep them there for the rest of the night. If he's found a loophole, I want to know it. If he's hidden in the buildings, he'll have to come out sometime. Get some men to search the roofs, and you and I can start on the alleyways. If he's out there, we'll get him." He straightened his shoulders and the sullen fire was back in his eyes—an angry, bitter fire. "And if he's gone into the Center, we'll still get him."

Bahr's eyes were wide. "He'll never come out if he's gone where you think, Jeff. We could wait weeks or months, even years, and we still wouldn't know. Even if he did come out, we might never recognize him."

"I'll recognize him," Jeff snarled, looking down into Bahr's face. "I'm going to kill him. I'm going to know that he's dead, because I'll see him die. And I'll kill him if I have to follow him into the Center to do it."

CHAPTER TWO

The news report blatted in Jeff Meyer's ear from the little car radio. The words came through, but he hardly heard them as his eyes watched the huge glass doors of the administration building of the Hoffman Medical Center.

... no word has yet been received, but it is believed that the Eurasian governments may be in session several hours more in an attempt to stem the inflation. On the home front, the stock-market nosedive, which resulted from the new Senate taxation bill yesterday, leveled off when the Secretary of Corporative Business announced this morning that the government would abandon attempts to enforce the new law, at least for the time being. Secretary Barnes stated that further study of the bill would be undertaken when more pressing governmental problems had been cleared—

Jeff snapped off the switch with a snarl. The street passing the Center was crowded. Lines of cars moved into and out of the traffic stream from the huge Center parking tiers. The building rose high, tier upon tier. Its walls gleamed white in the bright morning sunlight, reflecting brilliant facets of golden light from thousands of polished windows.

It was an immense building, sprawling across six perfectly landscaped city blocks, tall trees and cool green terraces setting off the glistening beauty of the architecture. The structure sent tower after tower up from the dingy street below, and at the foot of the towers was a buzz of furious activity. Supply trucks, carrying food and supplies for the twenty-two thousand beds and the people in them, and for the additional thirteen thousand people who worked day and night to keep the huge hospital running, moved toward the unloading platforms.

The Hoffman Medical Center was an age-old dream which had finally come true. Even those who had conceived it had not realized the tremendous need it would fulfill. From its very inception, no expense had been spared. The finest architects had thrown up the shimmering ward-towers, turned toward the sun, to bring light to the sick and injured who rested and healed within. Equipment unequaled anywhere in the world had filled the Center's dressing and surgical rooms. The doctors, nurses, researchers and technicians who staffed the institution had been

14

gathered from the world over. And all the world had conceded the Hoffman Center its place as leader in the realm of medicine, ever since the cornerstone had been laid that rainy morning in the spring of the year 2085. Twenty-four years had passed since that day, and in those years the Hoffman Center had never once faltered in its leadership.

The men in the car sat in stony silence. Finally, Jeff Meyer stirred, extended his hand briefly to Ted Bahr. "You'll cover things out here?"

"Don't worry about it." Bahr shook the hand. "Well wait to hear from you." He watched, almost wistfully, as the huge man cut through the traffic and headed for the large glass doors. Then, with a sigh, he stepped on the starter button and snaked the little jet car into the stream of traffic moving toward the city.

*

Jeff Meyer stopped in the great, bustling lobby and stared about him almost in awe. He had never been inside the Hoffman Center before, though he had heard of it many times and in many places. Since it had taken over service of the huge metropolis of Boston-New Haven-New York-Philadelphia, the newspapers and TV had been full of stories of the lifesaving and healing that had gone on within its walls. The disease research, conducted by specialists in all phases of medicine who were for the first time gathered together under one agency, had startled the world again and again.

But there had been other stories, too—not from the papers and TV, not these stories. These tales had come by word of mouth: a short sentence or two, a nervous laugh, a sneering joke, a rumor, a whispered story from a wide-eyed alky hanging over a bar. Not the sort of stories one really believed, but the sort that made one wonder.

Several dozen white-garbed women moved across the floor of the huge lobby and talked quietly among themselves. Jeff sniffed uneasily. There was a curiously distasteful odor in the air, an odor of almost unhealthy cleanliness and spotless preservation. The lobby was a mill of activity: the elevators and interbuilding jitneys terminated here; people moved briskly, carrying with them the familiar air of hurry and vast pressure that infected the whole world outside.

Jeff watched, spotting the corridor leading to the main administrative offices. He saw the elevators constantly rising to and returning from the

15

huge admission offices. He noted the corridor twisting off to the staff living quarters. He stood silent, his quick gray eyes cautiously probing and watching. He tried to print an indelible picture in his mind of the layout of the building and was almost floored by the hive-like bustle of the place. There was a complexity in the curved doorways and the brightly lighted corridors.

Somewhere here he could find Paul Conroe. Somewhere in this maze of buildings and passageways was the man he had hunted for. Logic told him that. They had spent the night searching every possible alternative. His muscles ached and his eyes were red from sleeplessness, but there was a hot, angry glow in his heart. He knew that this was the only place that Conroe could have gone. Yet the place where he must be hiding was a place Jeff had heard of only in rumor, a place whose mention carried with it a half-knowledge of staggering wealth and almost indescribable horror.

Someone tapped him on the shoulder. He turned, startled, to face a huge, burly man with a suspicious face and a gray uniform. "You got business here, mister, or are we just sight-seeing?"

Jeff forced a grin. "I don't know where to go," he said truthfully.

"Maybe you should go back out then. No visitors until this afternoon."

"No, I'm not a visitor. I'm looking for the Volunteer's Bank. The ads said to come to the administration offices—"

The guard's face softened a little. He pointed a finger toward a corridor marked RESEARCH ADMINISTRATION. "Right over there," he said. "Office is the first door to your right. The nurse will take care of you."

Meyer strolled toward the corridor, his mind fumbling with the rumors and bits of half-knowledge that were all that he had to work on: stories of drunks stumbling into the Emergency Rooms and never coming out; tales of quiet, swift raids on narcotics houses, of people who never reached the police stations.

But how could he make the right contact here? "Research Administration" covered a multitude of meanings. He had read the advertisements for Hoffman volunteers in all the buses, in the 'copters, on the roads. Newspapers and TV had carried them for years. Meyer glanced down at his unpolished shoes, rubbed a finger over his purposely unshaven chin. What would they expect a volunteer to look like? How could they detect a fraud, an interloper? He shivered as he faced the office door. It would be a gamble, a terrible chance. Because with all the other publicity, no mention had ever been made of the Mercy Men. He glanced back, found the guard still staring at him, and walked into the office.

Several people sat along the wall. A small, mousy-looking man with a bald head and close-set eyes had just sat down in the chair before the desk. He waited for the prim-looking woman wearing a ridiculous little white hat to put down her pen. She didn't even glance up as Jeff took a seat, and she kept writing for several minutes before turning her attention to the little bald man. Then she looked up and gave a frosty smile at him. "Yes, sir?"

"Dr. Bennet asked me to come back today," the little man said. "Follow-up on last week's work."

"Name please?" The woman took his name and punched the button on a panel before her; an instant later a card flipped down in a slot. She checked it, made an entry and nodded to the man. "Dr. Bennet will be ready for you at eleven. You'll find magazines in the lounge." She indicated another door, and the little man disappeared through it.

Another person, a middle-aged woman, moved to take the little man's place before the desk. Jeff felt restless and glanced at his watch. It was almost eleven. Must she move so slowly? Nothing seemed to hurry her. She worked from person to person, smiling, impersonal, just a trifle chilly. Finally she nodded to Jeff, and he moved to the chair.

"Name, please?"

"You don't have a card on me."

She looked up briefly. "A new volunteer? We're happy to have you, sir. Now if you'll give me your name, I can start the papers through."

Jeff cleared his throat, felt his pulse pounding in his forehead. "I'm not sure just what I want to volunteer for," he said cautiously.

The woman smiled. "We have a rather large selection to choose from. There are the regular 'mycin drug runs every week on Tuesdays and Thursdays. You take the drug by mouth in the morning and give blood samples at ten, two and four. Many of our new Volunteers start on that. It pays six dollars and your lunch while you're here. Or you could give blood, but the law restricts you to once every three months on that, and it only pays thirty-five dollars. Or—"

Jeff shook his head and leaned forward. He looked directly into her eyes. "I don't think you understand," he said softly. "I want money. Lots of it.

17

Not five or ten dollars." He looked down at the desk. "I've heard you have other kinds of work."

The woman's eyes narrowed. "There are higher-paying categories of Volunteer work, of course. But you must understand that they are higher paying because they involve a greater risk to the health of the Volunteer. For instance, we've been running circulation studies with heart catheterizations. We pay a hundred dollars for these, but there is an appreciable risk involved. Or sternal marrow punctures for blood studies. Usually we start—"

"I said money," said Jeff implacably. "Not peanuts."

Her eyes widened and she stared at him for a long moment. It was a strange, penetrating stare that took him in from his face to his feet. Her smile faded and her fingers were suddenly nervous. "Have you any idea what you're talking about?"

"I have. I'm talking about the Mercy Men."

She stood up abruptly and disappeared into an inner office. Jeff waited, his whole body trembling. Beads of sweat broke out on his forehead, and he gave a visible start when the woman opened the door again.

"Come in here, please."

Then he was on the right track. He tried to conceal the excitement in his eyes as he took a seat in the small room. He waited, fidgeting. The woman packed up a small telephone on the desk and punched several buttons in rapid succession. The silence was almost intolerable as he waited, a silence that was alive and vibrant. Finally a signal light flickered and she took up the receiver.

"Dr. Schiml? This is the Volunteer office, Doctor." She shot Jeff a swift glance. "There's another man here to see you."

Meyer felt his heart pound. He shifted in his chair and started to take out a cigarette. Then he checked himself.

"That's right," the woman was saying, eyeing him as if he were a biological specimen. "I'm sorry, he hasn't given a name.... Ten minutes? All right, Doctor, I'll have him wait." With that, she replaced the receiver and left the room without a word.

Jeff stood up, stretched his legs and looked about the room. It was small, with just a desk and two or three chairs. Obviously it served as a conference room of some sort. One wall held the panel of file buttons;

another held the telephone and visiphone viewer. Over the visiphone screen, a large lighted panel announced the date in sharp black letters: 32 April, 2109. Below it, the little transistor clock had just changed to read 11:23 A.M. Almost noon. And every passing minute his quarry drew farther and farther away.

He glanced out the window at the rising tiers of buildings. Across the courtyard the first of the ward-towers rose. To one side of it were a series of long, low structures with skylights. These were the kitchens, perhaps, or maintenance buildings. There were dozens of them—any one of which could be hiding Paul Conroe. Jeff clenched his hands until the nails bit his palms. He stared down at the buildings. Conroe could be anywhere down there. *Another man had already seen Dr. Schiml....*

A door clicked behind him and he turned sharply. A man entered the room and closed the door behind him. Smiling, he walked over to the desk. Meyer nodded and watched the man. He felt a sinking feeling in the pit of his stomach. For the briefest instant the doctor had caught his eye, and Jeff felt everything that he had planned to say crumble like dust around him.

The man hardly looked like a doctor, although his white jacket was immaculate and a stethoscope peeped from his side pocket. He was tall and slender, almost fifty years old, with round, cheerful pink cheeks and a little pug nose that seemed completely out of place on his face.

A harmless-looking man, Jeff thought, except for his eyes. But his eyes—they were the sharpest, most penetrating eyes Jeff had ever seen. And they were watching him. Quite independent of the smiling face, they watched his every move, studying him. The eyes were full of wisdom, but they were also tinged with caution.

The doctor sat down and motioned Jeff to the seat facing the desk. He pushed a cigar case across the desk to him.

Jeff hesitated, then took one. "I thought these were slightly illegal," he said.

The doctor grinned. "Slightly. Thanks to us, as you probably know. We did most of the work here on tobacco smoke and cancer—actually got legislation pushed through on it." He leaned back easily in his chair as he lit his own cigar. "Still, one once in a while won't do too much harm. And there's nothing like a good smoke to get things talked out. I'm Roger Schiml, by the way. I didn't get your name."

"Meyer," said Jeff. "Jeffrey Meyer."

The doctor's eyes narrowed quizzically. "I hope my girl didn't bother you too much. She channels most of the volunteer work here, as you see. Then, occasionally, cases come in which she'd rather turn over to me." He paused for a moment. "Cases like yours, for instance."

Jeff blinked, his mind racing. It would take acting, he thought, real acting to fool this man. The face was deceptively young and benign, almost complacent. But the eyes were far from young. They were old, old eyes. They had seen more than eyes should see. They missed nothing. To fool a man with eyes like that—Jeff took a deep breath and said, "I want to join the Mercy Men."

Dr. Schiml's eyes widened very slightly. For a long moment he said nothing, just stared at the huge man before him. Then he said, "That's interesting. It's also very curious. The name, I mean—oh, I can understand the attraction such an idea might have for people, but the name that's become so popular—it baffles me. 'Mercy Men.' It gives you a curious feeling, don't you think? Brings up mental pictures of handsome young interns fighting the forces of evil and death, the brave heroes giving their all for the upward flight of humanity—all that garbage, you know." The eyes hardened quite suddenly. "Where did you hear of the Mercy Men, I wonder?"

Jeff shrugged. "The word's been around for quite a while. A snatch here, a story there—even though it isn't advertised too openly."

Dr. Schiml looked him straight in the eye. "And suppose I told you that there is no such organization, either here or anywhere else on Earth that I know of?"

A tight smile appeared on Jeff's face. "I'd call you a class-A liar."

Schiml's eyebrows went up. "I see. That's a big word. Maybe you can support it."

"I can. There are Mercy Men here. There have been for several years."

"You're sure of that."

"Quite. I know one. He was a skid-rower with a taste for morphine when I first ran into him—a champagne appetite to go with a beer income. Then he went out of circulation for about six months. Now he has a place up in

ALAN E. NOURSE

the Catskills, with many, many thousands of dollars in the bank. Of course, he uses the money to feed several hundred cats in his basement." Jeff's eyes narrowed. "He never liked cats very much before he left here. There are other funny things he does—nothing serious, of course, but peculiar. Still, he doesn't need the dope any more."

Schiml smiled and put his fingers together. "That would be Luke Tandy. Yes, Luke was a little different when he left, but the work was satisfactory and we paid off."

"Yes," said Jeff softly. "One hundred and fifty thousand dollars. Cash on the line. To him or his heirs. He was lucky."

"So what are you doing here?"

"I want a hundred and fifty thousand dollars too."

The doctor's eyes met Jeff's squarely. "And you are a liar too."

Jeff reddened. "What do you mean—"

"Look, let's get this straight right now. Don't lie to me. I'll catch you every time." The doctor's eyes were hard. "I see a man who's eaten well for a long time, wearing dirty but expensive clothes, who doesn't drink, who doesn't use drugs, who is young and strong and capable. He tells me he wants to join the Mercy Men for money. He tells me a lie. Now I'll ask you again: why are you here?"

"For money. For one hundred and fifty thousand dollars."

The doctor sighed and leaned back. "All right, no matter. We'll go into it later, I suppose. But I think you'd better understand certain things. It's no accident that your information on the Mercy Men is so vague. We've been careful to keep it that way, of course. The more vague the stories, the fewer curiosity-seekers and busybodies we have to contend with. Also, the more distasteful the stories, the more desperate people will become before they come to us. This we particularly desire. Because the work we do here requires a very desperate man to volunteer."

As he talked, the doctor brought out a pack of cards from the desk and began riffling them nervously in his fingers. Jeff's eyes caught them and a chill went down his back. They were curious cards, not the regular playing variety. These were smaller, with a peculiar marking system in bright red on the white faces. Jeff shivered and he was puzzled at the chill that gripped his body. He shifted in his chair in growing tension and tried to take his eyes from the cards.

21

A MAN OBSESSED

The doctor snubbed out his cigar, leaned back in the chair and gave the cards a riffle and regarded Jeff closely. "We've done a lot here since the Center opened—work based on years of background research. A century or more ago there were terrible medical problems to be faced: polio was a killer then; they had no idea of cancer control; they were faced with a terrific death rate from heart disease. All those things are beaten now, a thing of the past. But as the old killers moved out, new ones took their place. Look at the half-dozen NVI plagues we've had in the past few years—neurotoxic virus infections that started to appear out of nowhere twenty years ago. Look at the alky-sikys you see in every bar today, a completely new type of alcoholism-psychosis that we haven't even been able to describe, much less cure. Look at the statistics on mental disease, rising in geometric progression almost every year."

The tall doctor stood up and walked to the window. "We don't know why it's happening, but it is. Something's on the march, something ghastly and evil among the people. Something that has to be stopped." He gave the cards a sharp riffle and tossed them onto the desk with a sigh. "We can't stop it until we know something about the human brain and how it works, and why it does what it does, and how. We don't even understand fully the structure of the nervous system, much less understand its function. And we've learned all we can from cats and dogs and monkeys. Any further study of a monkey's brain will give us great insight into the neuroses and complexes of monkeys, no doubt. But it won't teach us anything more about *men*." His voice was very soft. "You can see where this leads, I think."

Jeff Meyer nodded slowly. "You need men," he said.

"We need men. Men to study. Cruel as it may sound, men to experiment upon. We can't learn any more from any other variety of ... experimental animal. But there are problems. Toy around with a man's brain and he is likely to die, quite abruptly. Or he may be deranged, or he may go violently insane. Most of the work, however well planned, however certain we were of results, however safe it appeared, proved to be completely unpredictable. Much of the work and many of the results were quite horrible. But we're making progress, slow—but progress nonetheless. So the work continues.

"It hasn't been very popular. No man in his right mind would volunteer for such a job. So we hired men. For the most truly altruistic work in the world, our workers come with the most mercenary of motives: we pay for their services and we pay well. A hundred thousand dollars is a small fee, on our scale. We have the government behind us. The sky is the limit, if we need a man for a job. The money is paid, when the work is completed, either to the man himself or to his heirs. You see why the name they've given themselves is so curious—Medical Mercenaries, the 'Mercy Men.' That's why a man must be desperate to come to us. That's why we must be so very careful who joins us, for what motives."

Jeff Meyer stared at his hands and waited in the silence of the room. His eyes strayed once again to the curious cards, and the chill of fear went through him like a ghastly breeze. This was a port of last resort, a road that could end in horror and death. Ted Bahr had said it wasn't worth it—that Conroe would never escape alive—but he knew that Conroe could. And he knew Conroe well enough to know that he would.

Jeff felt the old bitterness and hatred swell up in his mind, and his hands trembled as he sat. He had long since thrown aside his life as he had known it, cast off the veneer of civilized life that he had acquired, to hunt Paul Conroe down and kill him. There was nothing else in his life that mattered. It had been a long, grueling hunt, tracking him, following him, studying him, tracing his movements and habits, plotting trap after trap, driving the man to desperation. But there had been no indication, anywhere along the line, that Conroe would turn to such a desperate gamble as this.

But he must have known that death otherwise was inevitable. Here he could be changed. He might disappear from the face of the Earth in the oblivion of quiet death, to be sure, but he also might emerge, unscathed, to live in wealth the rest of his life, unrecognizable and safe.

Jeff Meyer looked up at the doctor and his eyes were hard. "I haven't changed my mind," he said. "What has to be done to join?"

Dr. Schiml sighed, and turned resignedly to the file panel. "There are tests that are necessary and rules to be obeyed. You'll be confined and regimented. And once you're assigned to a job and sign a release, you're in." He leaned forward and punched the visiphone button. Tapping his fingers idly on the desk, he waited until an image blinked and cleared on the screen. "Blackie," he said tiredly. "Better send the Nasty Frenchman up here. We've got a new recruit."

The visiphone snapped off and Jeff sat frozen to his seat, his pulse throbbing in his neck, every nerve in his body screaming in excitement. The face on the screen had been clearly visible for a moment: a pale face with large gray eyes—a woman's face, surrounded by flowing black hair. It was a face that was impressed indelibly on his memory. It belonged to the girl who had danced the night before in the red light.

CHAPTER THREE

There was no doubt of it. She was the girl in the night club, the dancing girl with the flowing black hair and the mask-like smile, who had led him to Conroe and then brought the spotlight to his face to spring the trap too soon. Frantically Jeff fought to control his excitement. He knew his face was white and he avoided the doctor's puzzled glance. But he couldn't control the angry fire burning in his mind, the little voice screaming out: "*He's here; he's here, somewhere!*"

But why was she here? The doctor had called her "Blackie." He had spoken to her with familiarity. Jeff's mind whirled. He had the strangest feeling that he had missed something somewhere along the line, that he knew the answer but couldn't quite grasp it. What could the girl's sudden appearance in the Center involve?

Or had her appearance at the night club been the unusual one?

A buzzer rang and the office door opened to admit a small, weasel-faced man. The doctor looked up and smiled. "Hello, Jacques. This is Jeff Meyer, the new recruit. Take him down and get him quartered in, all right? And you might brief him a little. He's awfully green."

The little man scratched his long nose and regarded Jeff with a nasty smile. "A new one, huh? Where are you going to line him up?"

"No telling. We'll see where the tests put him, first. Then we'll talk about jobs."

The smile widened on the little man's face, turning down the end of his long pointed nose and revealing a dirty yellow row of teeth. His eyes ran over Jeff from head to toe. "Big one too. But then, they fall just as hard as the rest. Want me to take him right down?"

Schiml nodded. "Maybe he can still get lunch." His eyes shifted to Jeff. "This is the Nasty Frenchman," he said, motioning toward the little man with his thumb. "He's been around for a long time; he can show you the ropes. And don't let him bother you too much—his sense of humor, I mean. Like I say, he's been around here a long time. You'll get quarters and you'll be expected to stay with your group for meals and everything else. That means no contacts outside the hospital as long as you're here. You'll get the daily news reports, and there are magazines and books in the library. If you've got other business outside, you haven't any business in here. Any time you leave the Center it's considered an automatic breach of contract."

He paused for a long moment and gave Jeff a strange look, almost a half smile. "And you'll find that questions aren't appreciated around here, Jeff. Any kind of questions. The men don't like people too much when they ask questions."

The Nasty Frenchman shuffled his feet nervously, and Jeff started out the door. Then the little man turned back to Dr. Schiml. "They brought Tinker back from the table about ten minutes ago. He's in pretty bad shape. Maybe you should look at him?"

"This was the big job today, wasn't it?" Schiml's eyes were sharp. "What did Dr. Bartel say?"

"He said no dice. It was a bust."

"I see. Well, it may be just the diodrax wearing off now, but I'll be down to see."

The Nasty Frenchman grunted and turned back to Jeff. His face still wore the nasty little grin. "Let's go, big boy," he said, and started down the hall.

*

Jeff watched the corridors as they passed, counting them one by one, trying desperately to keep himself oriented. He glanced at his watch and angrily sucked in his breath. Minutes were slipping by, precious minutes, minutes that could mean success or failure. A thousand questions crowded his mind, and behind them all was the girl. She was the key, he was sure of it. She would know where Conroe was, where he could be found....

They reached an elevator, stepped aboard and shot down at such dizzying speed that Jeff nearly choked. Then, suddenly, they came to a jolting stop and stepped into a dingy, gray corridor that was dimly lit by bare bulbs in the ceiling.

The Nasty Frenchman punched a button in the wall and turned to regard Jeff. The sneering little smile was still on his lips as the far-off rumble of a jitney grew to a sharp clatter. A little car dropped down from its ceiling track. The little man hopped in nimbly and motioned Jeff in beside him. Then the car took off for the ceiling again, swinging crazily and speeding down the maze of corridors and curves.

Jeff stirred uneasily, growing more and more confused with every turn. "Look," he broke out finally, "where's this thing taking us?"

26

The Nasty Frenchman turned pale eyes toward him. "You worried or something?"

"Well, it looks like we're headed for the center of the Earth. I'd like to be able to find my way out sometime—"

"Why?"

The question was so blunt that it left Jeff's jaw sagging for a moment. "Well, I'm not planning to spend the rest of my life in here."

The Nasty Frenchman guffawed. It was not a pleasant laugh. "Here for a nice restful vacation, huh? You wise guys are all the same. Go ahead, dream—I won't bother you."

The little man turned his attention to the controls and the car swung sharply to the right and headed down another corridor. Jeff scowled as he watched the lighted corridors flash by. Were they speeding so far, so deep in the depths of the building? Or was this part of a definite plan to confuse, to lose recruits in the mammoth place so completely that they could never find their way out? Jeff shrugged, finally. It really didn't matter too much. He had one job and only one. He could worry about escape when it had been accomplished.

"That girl," he said finally. "The doctor called her 'Blackie.' Is she down here where we're going?"

"How should I know? I don't keep her on a leash." The little man's face darkened and his eyes turned suspiciously to Jeff.

"I mean, is she one of the group—one of the Mercy Men?"

The Nasty Frenchman threw a switch sharply, swerving the speeding car through a long, dim passage. He ignored the question, as if he hadn't heard it. In the dim light his skin was pasty yellow and wrinkled like a mummy. The cruelty and avarice on his face was frightening.

Jeff watched him for a moment or two, then said, "What brought you here? To the Mercy Men, I mean?"

The Nasty Frenchman's eyes flashed poisonously, his face a horrid mask. "Did I ask you your racket before you came in?"

"No."

"Then don't ask me mine. And you won't forget that, if you're smart." He turned his attention sharply to the controls, ignoring Jeff for several moments. Finally he said, "You'll share a room and you'll eat at eight, noon and six. Tests should start tomorrow morning at eight-thirty. You'll be in your room when the doctors come for you. You won't have any status here until you're tested. Then you'll sign a release and wait for a job assignment. You won't have any choice of work; that's just for the older ones. Some of the work is with central nervous system, some is with sympathetic; some work concentrates on spinal cord and peripherals, but most of the interest these days is in cortical lesions and repair. That pays the best, too—couple hundred thousand at a crack, with a fairly good risk."

"And what's a fairly good risk in here?"

The grin reappeared on the little man's face again. It was almost savage in its cruelty. "Ten per cent full recovery is a good risk. That means complete recovery from the work, no secondary infection, complete recovery of faculties—in other words complete success in the work. Then a *fairly* good risk runs slightly lower—more casualty, maybe five per cent recovery. And a high-risk job averages two per cent—"

The grin broadened. "You've got a better chance of living sitting under an atom bomb, my friend. And once you sign a release, relieving the hospital and the doctors of all responsibility, you're in, and held to your contract by law. This is no vacation, but if you're lucky enough to come through—" The little man's eyes were bright with eagerness. "They pay off—oh, how they pay off. If you're lucky, you'll get a good starter, maybe a hundred thousand, with good risk." He scratched his nose and regarded Jeff closely. "Of course, there are incomplete recoveries, too. They have trouble keeping them out of the news, if they ever leave. Pretty messy, sometimes, too."

Jeff felt his face paling at the cruel eagerness in the little man's voice. What could bring a man to a place like this—especially this kind of a man? Or had he been a different kind of a man before he came in? How long had he been here, waiting from experiment to experiment, waiting to live or to die, waiting for the payoff, the Big Cash that waited at the end of a job? What could such an existence do to a man? What could there be to drive him on? Jeff shuddered, then gasped as the car gave a sudden lurch around a corner and settled to the floor.

The Nasty Frenchman hopped out, motioned to Jeff to follow. They started walking toward the escalator at the end of the passageway. Jeff searched each doorway they passed, keeping alert for a sign of the black-haired woman. "Look," he said finally. "This girl—Blackie, I mean—who is she?"

The Nasty Frenchman stopped in his tracks, glared at Jeff. "What is she, an old family friend or something? You keep asking about her."

"I know her from somewhere."

"So why bother me with your questions?"

Jeff's face darkened angrily. "I want to see her, all right? Don't get so jumpy—"

The little man whirled on him like a cat. Jeff's arm was wrenched behind his back until he felt the tendons rip. With unbelievable strength the Nasty Frenchman twisted the huge man back against the wall and glared up at him with blazing eyes. "You're a smart guy, coming around here, asking questions," he snarled, giving Jeff's arm a vicious wrench. "You think you can fool me? You ask about this, you ask about that—why so nosey? Blackie ... me ... everything. What are you doing here? Going after the Big Cash or asking questions?"

"The Cash!" Jeff gasped. He twisted to wriggle free of the iron-like grip.

"Then don't ask questions! We don't like nosey people here; we like people that roll dice square and mind their own business." The little man gave the arm a final agonizing wrench and released it. He jumped back, poised, eyes savagely eager.

Every instinct screamed at Jeff to rush him, but he slumped against the wall. Rubbing his aching arm, he fought for control. He knew a fight now could ruin things completely. Already he had blundered terribly. He cursed under his breath. How stupid he'd been not to have realized how unpopular questions would be to people in a place like this. And surely the word would get to the girl now that he was asking about her. Unless he could get to her first—

Still rubbing his elbows painfully, he turned to the Nasty Frenchman. "Okay, let it go," he growled. "Where do we go from here?"

The room was small and barren. Dingy and gray, it matched Jeff's spirit perfectly. He entered it with the Nasty Frenchman at his heels and stared at the two stark hospital beds against the far wall, the two foot lockers, the two small desk-and-chair combinations. There was no window in the room. Indeed, there was nothing about the room or corridor to prove that they were not twenty miles underground. Certainly the jitney ride had been no reassurance to the contrary.

The dim wall lights glowed on scrubbed, peeling paint, and the floor was covered with clean but well-worn plastic matting. Against one wall was a TV set. Between the beds a door led into a compact lavatory and shower. Glancing in, Jeff saw the lavatory was also connected with the adjoining room.

"It's no Grand Hotel," the Nasty Frenchman said sourly. "But it's clean and it's a bed. This corridor quarters your whole unit—the C unit. Other units are on other floors, up and down."

Jeff looked around the room gloomily. "Where can I eat?"

"The mess hall's four flights down. Take the escalator at the end of the hall. It closes in half an hour, so you'd better step on it. And if you're smart, you won't go wandering around. These boys in gray you see here and there don't like us very much." His face creased into a sardonic grin as he started for the door. "And you'd be smart to change before you come down. The faster people stop thinking you're new here, the happier you'll be." With that, he turned and disappeared down the hall.

Jeff gave a sigh, and prowled the room. One of the foot lockers held an amazing assortment of clean and dirty clothes. On the floor of it lay a large heap of dirty shirts and trousers, and nested squarely in the center of the pile was a heap of gold rings and wrist watches. Jeff blinked, not quite believing his eyes. He hadn't thought to ask about his room-mate, but apparently he had one who had not yet made his appearance.

Apparently everyone wore similar clothing. He found the other locker filled with clean shirts and dungarees. Swiftly he started to change, his mind racing. His body was sore all over and he felt a dry, hot feeling around his ears from lack of sleep. His arm ached miserably every time he moved it. If only he could sleep for a little while. But he knew there was no time to be wasted. In the mess hall there would still be people. Somewhere among them he would find the girl....

Carefully he considered the problem. The girl was the key. He had to find her, to make certain that Conroe was here. And he had to find her quickly, catch her unawares, before she had a chance to alibi or hide. Conroe would be hidden; he would never come into the open until he was sure that he had not been followed. He too must be taken unawares. Jeff had seen Conroe slip out of too many traps in the past. A blunder now could be the last. And if Conroe had time to plan, there would be many, many blunders.

A car buzzed down the hall as he stood in the room and stopped a little way from the door. There were voices, subdued, yet carrying a sharp note of frantic excitement. Jeff paused, listening to the combination of unfamiliar sounds: a grunt, a low curse, a rustle of whispered conversation, a low whistle. Then the door to the next room banged open and a rumble and squeak of wheels came to his ears.

"Jeez, what a job!"

"Yeah, looks bad. Did the doc see him?"

"He said he'd be down—"

"—gotta let it wear off before you can tell. This was the works, this time."

Jeff walked quietly to the door of the connecting lavatory, his nerves tingling. A new sound was apparent, an unearthly sound of labored, gurgling breathing. Jeff shivered. He had heard a sound like that only once before in his life: in a rocket during the Asian war, when a man had been struck in the throat with a chunk of shrapnel. Carefully, he pushed the door open an inch, peered through....

There were three men standing in the room, maneuvering a man—if it was a man—from the four-wheeled cart onto the bed. The man's head was covered to the shoulders with bandage. A patch of fresh blood showed near the temple, and a rubber tube emerged where the mouth should have been.

"Got him down? Better cover him closer. Restrainers—he may jump around. Doc said three weeks for shock to wear off, if he makes it through the night."

"Yeah—and this is the Big Cash for Tinker too. Harpo nearly beat him to the job, but Schiml had promised him—"

Jeff shuddered. This, then, was one of the Mercy Men, finished with a "job." The gurgling sound grew louder, measuring itself with the man's breathing—short, shallow, a measure of death. An experiment had been completed.

Jeff closed the door silently. His face in the mirror was pasty white and his hands were shaking. Here was the factor that had been plaguing him from the start, finally breaking through to the surface. The road he was traveling was a one-way road. He had to find Conroe and get off the road quickly, while he could. *Because he dared not travel the road too far....*

*

The air in the corridor seemed fresher as Jeff started for the escalator. It was almost two o'clock and he hurried, anxious to reach the mess hall before it closed. He consciously fought the picture of the man on the bed out of his mind. With effort he focused his attention once again on the girl. At the end of the corridor he stepped onto the creaky, down-going escalator.

If only he could check with Ted Bahr, make certain that the trail had really ended at the Hoffman Center, make sure that Conroe was not really somewhere outside, still hiding, still running. One thing seemed certain: if Conroe were really here, he too would be faced with the testing and classification; he too would be traveling the same grim road as Jeff himself. And as a newcomer, he too would be under suspicion and scrutiny.

Jeff stopped short on a landing. He was suddenly aware that he had lost count of the flights he had gone down. He looked back to check his bearings, then moved around to the stairs moving up. The escalator creaked and groaned, as if every turn would be its last, and Jeff stared dreamily at the moving wall, waiting—until he passed the open well to the opposite stairs.

He froze, his mind screaming. Unable to move, he stared at the pale, frightened face of the man on the down-going stairway. In the brief seconds while they passed, he stood rooted, paralyzed, unable to cry out. Then with a hoarse yell he turned. Half-stumbling, half-falling, he ran down the up-going stairs until he reached the opening.

Then he vaulted across the barrier, crashing his shoulder against the wall as he went through. He caught a glimpse of the tall, slender figure running from the bottom of the stairs into the corridor at the bottom, and he shouted again in a burst of blinding rage. He took the steps three at a time, his mind numb to the pain as his foot struck the solid floor and twisted, sending him sprawling on his face. In an instant he was on his feet again, running, frantically, blindly, to the end of the corridor.

It broke into two hallways, going off in a Y. Both were dark and both were empty. Jeff stood panting, almost screaming out in rage, his whole body trembling. He started blindly down one corridor, jerked open a door and stared in at the small, empty office. He tried another door and another. Then he turned and ran back to the Y, spun around the corner and ran pell-mell down the second corridor. Only his own desperate footfalls echoed back to him in the darkness.

Back at the Y, he sank to the floor. Still panting, he sobbed aloud in his rage, clenching his fists as he tried to regain control of his spinning mind. Rage there was—yes, and hatred and bitter frustration. But also, tumbling through his mind in a wild, elated cadence, was a cry of sheer, incoherent savage joy. Because he knew now, beyond any shadow of doubt, that Paul Conroe was among the Mercy Men.

He looked up suddenly at the two figures approaching him from the lighted corridor. One of them held a tiny, deadly scorcher pistol trained on his chest. The other, a huge, burly man, reached down and jerked Jeff's face up into the light. "What's your unit?" the harsh voice grated.

Jeff glimpsed the gray cloth of the man's jacket, the official-looking black belt over his shoulder. "C unit," he panted.

The blow caught him full on the chin, twisting his head around with a jolt. "Wise guy, wandering around without a pass," the voice growled. "You goddam scabs think you run the place, don't you?" Another blow struck him behind the ear, and a fist caught him hard in the pit of the stomach. As he doubled over retching, a smashing blow caught his chin, and he tasted blood in his mouth as his knees buckled under him.

*

He felt them, vaguely, half-carrying, half-dragging him down the corridor. He heard a door open and fell face down on the floor. A harsh voice said, "Here's your room-mate, scut. Keep him home from now on." And the door slammed behind him.

Painfully, he raised himself on his hands, shook his head dazedly.

"You look like you're sick or something." The voice from the bed was hard and insolent.

Painfully, Jeff jerked his head up and stared. The girl blinked coldly and pulled a frazzled cigarette from her blue cotton shirt. She flicked a match with her thumb and touched off the smoke. Then she stared down at Jeff mockingly. "Sorry, Jack," said the girl called Blackie. "But it looks like we're roomies. So you might as well get used to the idea."

CHAPTER FOUR

Something exploded in Jeff's brain then, something he could no more control than the creeping, vicious hatred of Paul Conroe that had driven him for so long. The jangling, tinny music of the tavern was screaming through his mind; the indelible picture of the swerving, gyrating figure: the long raven hair, the impassive face, the full lips. His knees buckled and his head was reeling, but he lurched across the room at the girl. Catching her by the collar, he drew her face up to his with a wrench that knocked the cigarette from her hand and brought her breath out in a gasp.

"All right," he grated. "Where is he? Come on, come on, talk! Where is he? And don't tell me he's not here, because I know he is, understand? I just saw him. I just chased him, down below. I know he's here! I want to know where."

Her foot came up sharply and caught him in the leg, sending an agony of pain into his thigh. Suddenly she began to fight like a cat, clawing, biting—blue fire in her eyes. Jeff brought his hand up and slapped her face twice, hard. With a snarl she caught him in the stomach with her foot and tore herself free, sending him reeling back against the wall.

He bounded off, then stopped dead in his tracks. A horrible realization exploded in his mind. She was standing poised, her face twisted, her eyes burning, a stream of poisonous language pouring at him. In her hand was a knife, blade up, balanced in her hand with deadly intent. But Jeff hardly noticed the knife; he didn't hear the words as he stared unbelievingly at her face, his heart sinking. Because the face was wrong, somehow.

The lips were not right, the nose was shaped differently, the glow in the eyes was not right. His panting turned into a bitter sob of disbelief, of incredible disappointment. There couldn't be any doubt—it simply was not the right girl.

"Where—where is he?" he asked weakly, his heart pounding helplessly in his throat.

"Not another step," the girl snarled. "Another inch and I'll slice you up like putty."

"No, no—" Jeff shook his head, trying desperately to clear his mind, to understand. This was the girl he had seen in the visiphone screen. Yes, the same clothes, the same face. But she wasn't the girl in the tavern. "Conroe," he blurted out, plaintively. "You—you must know Conroe—"

"I've never heard of Conroe."

"But you must have—last night, in that dive—dancing—"

Her jaw dropped as she stared at him in disgust. Then she gave the knife a flip into the desk top and sank down on her bed, her face relaxing. "Go away," she said tiredly. "That goddam Frenchman's sense of humor. Go on, beat it. I'm not rooming with any hoppy—at least until he's off the stuff."

"You don't know Conroe?"

The girl looked at him closely. "Look, Jack," she said with patient bitterness, "I don't know who you are and I don't know your pal Comstock or whatever it is. And I sure as hell wasn't dancing anywhere last night. I was working in the tank last night getting some looped-up hophead cooled off for the axe this morning. And it wasn't fun for either of us, and you'll be down there yourself if you don't cool off. And you won't like it, either. So go away, don't bother me."

Jeff sank down on the opposite bed, his head in his hands. "You—you looked so much like her—"

"So I looked so much like her!" She spat out a filthy word and drew her legs up, glaring at him.

Jeff reddened, his whole body aching. "All right, I'm sorry. I got excited. I couldn't help it. And I can't leave here—I tried it a little while ago and ran into a couple of fists."

Blackie's lip curled. "The guards don't like us down here. They don't like anything about us. They'll kill you if you give them half an excuse."

Jeff looked up at her. "But why? I didn't do anything."

The girl laughed harshly. "Do you think that makes any difference to them? Look, Jack, let's face it: you're in a prison, understand? They don't call it that, and there aren't any bars. But you're not going anywhere, and the boys in gray are here to see that you don't. And they hate us because we're not good enough for them, and we're in line for the kind of money they don't dare go after. You're here for one thing: to make money, big money, or to get your brains jolted loose, and nothing else—" She looked up at him, her eyes narrowing. "Or are you?"

Jeff shook his head miserably. "No, nothing else. I'm waiting for testing. This other thing is an old fight, that's all. You wouldn't understand. You just looked so much like the girl—" He looked up at her, studying her face more closely. She wasn't as young as he had thought at first. There were little wrinkles around her eyes, a shade too much make-up showing where her mouth crinkled when she talked. Her lips were painted too full, and there was a tiredness in her eyes, a beaten, hunted look that she couldn't quite hide.

She leaned back on the bed, and even relaxation didn't erase the hardness. Only the jet black hair and the smooth black eyebrows looked young and fresh.

Jeff shook his head and kept staring at her. "I don't get it," he said helplessly. "I was assigned to this room—"

"So was I." The girl's eyes hardened.

"Are you one of the ... workers?"

She sneered bitterly. "You mean one of the experimental animals? That's right. The Mercy Men. Full of mercy, that's me." She spat on the floor.

"But the mixed company—"

There was no humor in her laugh. "What did you think, they'd have a separate boudoir for the ladies? How do they treat any kind of experimental animal? Get off it, Jack. They don't care what we do or how we live. All they want is good healthy human livestock when they're ready for it. Nothing more. That means they have to feed us and bunk us down. Period. And if you've got any wise ideas"—her eyes widened with a look of open viciousness, shocking in its intensity—"just try something. Just once. You'll find out a lot about Blackie in a hell of a rush." She rolled over contemptuously, turning her back to him. "You'll find out I don't like loonies for roommates, for instance."

Jeff lit a cigarette, his hands trembling. The room seemed to be spinning, and he felt his muscles sagging in pain and fatigue. He had counted so much on information from the girl. But incredible as the resemblance was, Blackie couldn't have been the girl he had seen in the tavern. If she had recognized him, he would have spotted it. She couldn't have hidden it completely.

Suddenly he felt terribly alone, almost beaten, helpless to go on. Where could he go? What could he do? How could he follow a trail that led straight into stone walls? He leaned back on the bed and yielded to the fatigue that plagued him. His mind sank into a confusion of hopelessness. Maybe, he thought wearily, maybe that plaguing doubt that lay in the fringes of his mind was right. Maybe he'd never find Conroe. He sighed as the darkness of utter exhaustion closed in on him, and his head sank back to the pillow—

*

He knew he was dreaming. Some tiny corner of his mind stood aside, prodding him, telling him he dare not sleep, that he must be up, moving, hunting, that the danger was too grave for sleep. But he slept, and the little corner of his mind prodded and cried out and watched....

He was walking along a brook, a walk he had taken once before, so very many years ago. A cool breeze struck down from the meadow, rumpling his hair. He heard the tinkle of the water as it sparkled across the rock. And he was afraid, so desperately afraid. The voice in his mind screamed out to him at every footstep, until he faltered and slowed and stopped.

Not here, Jeff, not here. Stop, stop now! If you go farther, you'll be dead—

Sweat broke out on his forehead. He tried to move forward, felt an iron grip on his legs. *Stop, Jeff, stop, you'll die, Jeff—*An overpowering wave of fear swept over him, and he turned. He ran like the wind, with the voice following him, crying out in his ear, following him on ghostly wings. In the dream he became a little boy again, running, screaming in fear. A man stood in his pathway, arms outstretched, and Jeff threw himself into his father's arms, sobbing as though his heart would break, clutching at him with incredible relief, burying his face in the strong, comforting chest. *Oh, daddy, daddy, you're safe. You're here, daddy.*

He looked up at his father's smiling face and he saw the strong, sensitive lines around the big man's mouth, the power and wisdom in the eyes. Nowhere else was there this sense of strength, of unlimited power, of complete comfort. He buried his face again in old Jacob Meyer's chest. A flood of deep peacefulness passed through his mind—

Jeff, Jeff, watch out!

He stiffened, his whole body going cold. The strong arms were no longer around him, and he was suddenly afraid again—afraid with a terror that bit deep into his mind. He looked up and screamed, a scream that echoed and re-echoed. It came again and again—a scream of pure terror. Because his father's face was no longer next to him. There was another face, hanging bodiless and luminous above him. It was chalk white—a face of pure ghoulish evil, staring at him.

It was Conroe's face. He screamed again, tried to cover his eyes, tried to shrink down into nothing. But the hideous, twisted face followed him. The horrible fear intensified, sweeping through him like a flame, twisting into fiery hate in his heart, as he watched the evil, glowing face.

He killed your father, Jeff. He butchered your father, shot him down like an animal, in cold blood—

Jeff screamed and the evil face grinned and moved closer, until the rank breath was hot on Jeff's neck.

You must kill him, Jeff. He killed your father—

But why? Why did he do it, why ... why ... *why?* There was no answer. The voice trailed off into horrible laughter. Quite suddenly the face was gone. In its place was a tiny, distant figure—running, running like the wind, down the narrow, darkened hospital corridor. And Jeff was running too, burning with hatred, fighting desperately to catch up with the fleeing figure, to close the gap between them.

The walls were of gray stone. Conroe was running swiftly, unhindered. But horrid objects swept out of the walls at Jeff. He tripped on a wet, slimy thing on the floor and fell on his face. He scrambled up again as the figure disappeared around a far corner. The walls were gray and wet around him. He reached the Y, waiting, panting, screaming out his hatred down the empty, re-echoing hallways.

Then suddenly he glimpsed the figure and started running again, but they were no longer in the Hoffman Center. They were running down a hillside, a horrible, barren hillside, studded with long knives and spears and swords—shiny blades standing straight up from the ground, gleaming in the bluish light.

Conroe was far ahead, moving nimbly through the gauntlet of swords. But Jeff couldn't follow his path, for new knives sprang up before him, cutting his ankles, ripping his clothes. He panted, near exhaustion, as the figure vanished in the distance. Sinking down to the ground, Jeff sobbed, his whole body shaking. And the voice screamed mockingly in his ear: *You'll never get him, Jeff. No matter how hard you try, you'll never get him ... never ... never ... never....*

But I've got to, I've got to. I've got to find him and kill him. Daddy told me to—

He woke with a jolt, his screams still echoing in the still room, sweat pouring from his forehead and body, soaking his clothes. He sat bolt upright. He searched for his watch, but couldn't find it. *How long had he slept?*

His eyes shot to the opposite bed, standing empty, and he rolled out onto his feet. He had the horrible feeling that the world had passed him by, that he had missed something critical while he slept.

He stared at his wrist. The watch was definitely gone. Then, with a curse, he crossed the room and ripped open Blackie's foot locker. Sure enough, the watch lay with the heap of gold jewelry on the dirty clothes pile. He stared at it as he re-strapped it on his wrist. Then he walked into the lavatory, splashed cold water into his face and tried to quell the fierce painful throbbing in his head. The watch said eight-thirty. He had slept for five hours—five precious hours for Conroe to hide, cover his tracks, disappear deeper into this mire of human trash.

Jeff stumbled to the door, glanced out to see two gray-clothed guards passing in the corridor. Quietly he pulled the door shut. His stomach was screaming from hunger and he searched the room restlessly. Finally, he unearthed a box of crackers and a quarter pound of cheese in the bottom of Blackie's locker. He ate ravenously and drank some water from the lavatory tap. Then he sank down on the edge of the bed.

The dream again, the same horrible, frightening, desperate dream—the dream that recurred and recurred; always different, yet always the same. The same face that had haunted him all his life, the face that had almost driven him insane that day, five years before, when he met it face to face for the first time; the face of the man he had hunted to the ends of the earth. But never had he caught the man, never had he seen him but for brief glimpses. Conroe had slipped from every trap before it was sprung. Yet finally he had become so desperate that he was forced to retreat down a one-way road that led to hellish death.

Jeff shook his head hopelessly as he tried to piece together the situation. He was in a half-world of avaricious men and women out to sell themselves for incredible fees. It was a half-world that seemed to Jeff only slightly more insane than the warped, intense world of pressure and fear and insecurity that lay outside the Hoffman Center. And in this half-world were a doctor who knew Jeff was a fraud, a kleptomaniac girl who thought he was an addict, and somewhere—the slender figure of the man he hunted.

Again he walked to the door. After peering out cautiously, he started down the corridor. From the far end he heard a burst of laughter, the sound of many voices. The smell of coffee floated down the corridor to tantalize him. He followed the sounds and reached the large, long room that served as a lounge and library for the Mercy Men in his unit.

The room was crowded. A dozen groups were huddled on the floor in a buzz of frantic excitement. The room was blue with cigarette smoke, and the lights glowed harshly from the walls. He saw the dice rolling in the centers of the groups and he also saw half a dozen tables, crowded with bright-eyed people. He heard the riffle of playing cards and the harsh, tense laugh of a winner drawing in a pot. And then he spied the Nasty Frenchman, his eyes bright with excitement, a cup of exceedingly black coffee in one hand and a pile of white paper tags in the other.

He grinned at Jeff with undisguised malice and said, "Come on in, wise guy. Things are just beginning to get hot."

Blinking, Jeff walked into the room.

CHAPTER FIVE

His first impulse was to turn and run. There was no explaining it, no rationalizing the feeling of dread and danger that struck him as he walked into the room. The feeling swept over him with almost overpowering intensity; something was unbearably wrong here.

Jeff walked in slowly, closing the door behind him. The door seemed to be pulled tight shut, sucked out of his hand. That was when the tension in the air struck Jeff like an almost physical force, and his mind filled with dread.

No one noticed him. He stared around himself curiously. He watched the Nasty Frenchman shoulder his way through the crowd. One of Silly Giggin's particularly maddening nervous-jazz arrangements was squawking from a player somewhere in the room, and the air itself was filled with a jagged rattle of conversation that rose above the music.

Most of the faces were new to Jeff. There were tired, old ones, marked indelibly with lines of fear, lines of hunted hopelessness. There were faces with tight, compressed, bloodless lips; faces with eyes full of coldness and cynicism, and faces radiating sharp, perverted intelligence.

Crowds leaned tensely around the tables and watched the cards with eager, calculating eyes. Side bets were made as the hands were opened. Other groups huddled on the floor and watched the dice with beady, avaricious eyes.

The music jangled and scraped, and little bursts of harsh laughter broke out to compete with it. And through it all ran the chilling inescapable feeling of error, of something missed, something gone horribly wrong.

He moved slowly through the room and searched the faces milling around him. His eyes caught Blackie's, far across the room, for the barest instant, and the chill of something gone wrong intensified and sent a quiver up his spine. He stopped a passerby and motioned at the nearest dice huddle. "How do you get in?" he asked.

The man shrugged, looking at him strangely. "You lay down your money and you play," he snapped. "If you got no money, then you've got the next job's payoff to bet with. 'Smatter, Jack, you new around here?" And the man moved on, shaking his head.

41

Jeff nodded, realization striking. What would be more natural to a group of people teetering from day to day on the brink of death? The need for excitement, for activity, would be overpowering in a dismal prison-place like this. And with the huge sums of money yet unearned to bet with—Jeff shuddered. Cut-throat games, yes, but could they really explain this strange tension he sensed? Or had something happened, something to change the atmosphere, to pervade every nook and cranny of the room with an air of explosive tension?

Jeff started moving toward the Nasty Frenchman. The little man was gulping coffee in the corner. He sucked on a long, black cigar and appeared to be in deep conversation with a bald-headed giant who leaned against the wall. Jeff spotted Blackie again. She was across the room on her knees. She faced a little buck-toothed man, as she swiftly rolled the three colored dice. Her eyes followed them, quick and unnaturally bright.

Jeff shook his head. Panmumjon was a high-speed, high-tension game—a game for the steel-nerved. Its famous dead-locks had often led to murder, as the pots rose higher and higher. The girl seemed to be winning. She rolled the dice with trance-like regularity, and the little buck-toothed man's face darkened as his money pile dwindled.

Across the room a corner crap game was moving swiftly, with staggering sums of money passing from hand to hand; the card games, though slower, left the mark of their tension on the players' faces. Jeff still stared, until he had seen every face in the room. Paul Conroe's face was not one of them.

No, he had not expected that. But what had happened? It was maddening to stand there, to feel the tension in the room, sense that it was growing until it seemed to pound at his temples. No one else seemed to notice it. Was he the only one aware of the change in the air, in the sounds, even in the color of the light against the walls? Something was impelling him, urging him to run, to get away, to leave the room now while he could. Yet when he tried to analyze the creeping, poisonous fear, tried to pin it down, it wriggled away into the fringes of his mind, and mocked him.

Finally, he reached the corner of the room. His ear caught the Nasty Frenchman's nasal voice, and he froze as he stared at the little man.

"I tell you, Harpo, I heard it with my own ears. You never saw Schiml so excited. And then Shaggy Parsons was saying that the whole unit was being split up—that's the A unit. I saw him when I was going through this afternoon. He was all excited, too."

"But why split it up?" The huge bald-headed man called Harpo growled, his heavy lips twisting in disgust. "I don't trust Shaggy Parsons for nothin', and I think you hear what you want to hear. What's the point to it? Schiml's coming along fine in the work he's using us in—"

The Nasty Frenchman turned red. "That's just it: we've been in and we're going to be out, right out in the cold. Can't you get that straight? Something's going to break. They're onto something—Schiml and his boys—something big. And they've got a new man, somebody they're excited about, somebody that's been knocking walls down just by looking at them, or something—"

Harpo made a disgusted noise. "You mean, the old ESP story again. So maybe they go off on another spook hunt. They'll get over it, same as they did the last time or the time before."

The Nasty Frenchman's voice was tense. "But they're *changing things*. And changes mean trouble." He glanced at Jeff and his eyebrows went up. "Look, they get on a line of work, they assign men to different parts of a job, they get work lined up months in advance. Then all of a sudden something new comes along. They get excited about something and they toss out a couple dozen workers, add on a couple dozen new ones, change the fees, change the work. And they end up handing the best pay to somebody who's just come in. I don't like it. I've been in this place too long. I've had too many tough, lousy jobs here to just get pushed aside because they don't happen to be interested any more in what they were doing to me before. And they never tell us! We never know for sure. We just have to wait and guess and hope."

The little man's eyes blazed. "But we can pick up some things, a little here, a little there—you learn how, after a while. And I can tell you, something's wrong, something's going to happen. You can even feel it in here."

Jeff's skin crawled. That was it, of course. There was something wrong. But it hadn't happened yet. It was going to happen. He stared at a huddled group around a panmumjon game, watched the bright-colored dice cubes roll across and back, across and back. A newcomer, the Nasty Frenchman had said, someone who had come in and disrupted the smooth work schedule of the Center, someone who had the doctors suddenly excited. Someone whom they were planning to use—on a spook hunt.

What kind of a spook hunt? Why that choice of words? Could Conroe conceivably be the newcomer they had been talking about? It didn't seem possible that it could have happened so suddenly if Conroe were the one—but who? And what did this have to do with the ever-growing sense of impending danger that pervaded the room, right now?

Jeff's eyes wandered to the dice game, and the fear in his mind suddenly grew to a screaming torrent. *Go away, Jeff. Don't watch, don't look*—He scowled, suddenly angry. Why not look? What was there so dangerous in a dice game? He moved over to the nearby huddle and watched the moving cubes in fascination. *No, Jeff, no, don't do it, Jeff*—With a curse, he dropped to his knees and reached out for the dice.

"You in?" somebody asked. Jeff nodded, his face like a rock. The voice had stopped screaming in his ear, and now something else grew in his mind: a wild exhilaration that caught his breath and swept through his brain like a whirl-wind. His eyes sparkled and he pulled money from his pocket. He laid the bills on the floor and his hands closed on the dice.

He faced a little, pimple-faced man with beady black eyes and he raised the three brightly colored dice, rolling into the familiar pattern. The dice deadlocked in four throws. He sweated out seven more with new dice. Then Jeff saw a break in the odds, boosted the ante on his next throw and caught his breath as the man facing him matched it.

The dice rolled, fell into deadlock again, and the crowd around them gasped, moved in closer around them. The third set of dice was brought out, for the attempts at dead-lock-breaking. Then a fourth set followed, as the complex structure of the game built up like a house of cards. Then Jeff's dice at last rolled the critical number, and the structure began to break apart—throw after throw falling faster and faster into his hands.

Four or five people moved in at his side with side bets and began to collect along with him, as he moved into another game, built it up. This one he lost cold, but still he played on, his excitement growing.

And then, suddenly, pandemonium broke loose in the room. Eyes glanced up, startled, at the two men, far across the room, who stood facing each other, eyes blazing.

"Throw them down! Go on! Throw them, see how they land!"

Somebody shouted, "What happened, Archie?"

"He's got loaded dice in here, somehow." Archie pointed an accusing finger at the other man. "They don't fall right. There's something wrong with them—"

The other man snarled. "So you aren't winning any more—so what? You brought the dice in yourself."

"But the odds aren't right. There's something funny going on."

Jeff turned back to the dice, his mind still screaming, sensing that disaster hung in the air like a heavy sword. His own game moved on, faster and faster. Somewhere across the room another fight broke out, and another. Several men dropped out of games and stood up against the walls. Their eyes were wide with anger as they watched the other players. And then Jeff rolled three sixes, fourteen times in a row. He tossed the dice down in front of his gaping opponents with a curse and walked shakily back to the corner. The whole room spun around his head.

Suddenly, in this room, probabilities had gone mad. He could feel the shifting instability of the atmosphere, as real and oppressive to him as if it were solid and he were attempting to wade through it. This was what had been bothering him, plaguing him. Quite suddenly and without explanation, something impossible had begun to happen. Cards had begun to fall in unbelievable sequences, repeating themselves with idiotic regularity; dice had defied the laws of gravity as they spun on the tables and floor.

A hubbub filled the room as the players stopped and stared at each other, unable to comprehend the impossible that was happening before their eyes. And then Blackie was passing Jeff, her face flushed, a curious light of desperation in her eyes.

An impulse passed through Jeff's mind. He reached out an arm, stopped the girl. "Game," he said sharply.

Her eyes flashed at him. "What game?"

"Anything." He held up his wrist before her eyes and showed her the gold watch. "We can play for this."

Something flared in her eyes for a moment before she gained control. Then she was down on her knees, pushing her sleeves up, a tight look of fear and dread haunting her eyes as she looked up at Jeff. "Something's happening," she said softly. "The dice—they're not right."

"I know it. Why not?" His voice was hoarse, his eyes hard on her face.

She threw him a baffled look. "There isn't any reason. Nothing is different, but the dice don't fall right. That's all, they just don't."

Jeff grinned tightly. "Go on, throw them."

She threw the dice, saw them dance on the floor, caught her number. Jeff rolled them, beat her on it, picked up the money. He rolled again, then again. The tightness grew around the girl's eyes; little tense lines hardened near her mouth. Nervously, she fumbled a cigarette into her mouth, lit it, puffed as the dice rolled.

She lost. She lost again. Side bets picked up around them, the people as they watched catching the tension that was building up.

"What's happening?"

"The dice—my God! They've gone crazy!"

"Blackie's losing. What do you think—"

"—losing? She never loses on dice. Who's the guy?"

"Never saw him before. Look, he took another one! Those dice are hexed."

"My cards were crazy too: king high full every time, a dozen hands in a row. How can you bet on something like that, I ask you."

The Silly Giggins record screeched louder, then gave a squawk as the record suddenly shattered in a thousand pieces. Somebody cursed and threw a pack of cards on the floor, and a scream broke out across the room. One group came suddenly to blows; several dice games tightened down to bloody conflict between individuals. A man burst into tears, suddenly, and sat back on his haunches, his face stricken. "They can't act this way," he wailed. "They just can't—"

Jeff's eyes watched the spinning dice, and again something was screaming in his ear. He felt as though his head were going to burst, but he continued to roll and he saw the girl's face darken with each throw. He saw the fear shine out from her blue eyes. Suddenly she let out a curse, snatched the dice from Jeff's hand and threw them sharply across the room. She stared at Jeff venomously, then glared at the people around her as if she were a cornered animal.

"It's all of you," she snarled. "You're turning them against me. You're making them fall wrong." She spat on the floor and started for the door. Jeff moved after her but felt a restraining hand on his arm.

46

"Leave her alone," said the Nasty Frenchman. "You'll have trouble on your hands if you don't. You see what I meant about something being wrong? The whole crowd here is on edge, as if somebody were picking them up and throwing them down. Who ever saw dice fall that way, or cards fall that way"—the little man's eyes flashed slyly—" *unless somebody was controlling them.*"

Jeff's breath was faster as he stared at the Nasty Frenchman, and his voice was hoarse. "What are you talking about?"

The little man's lips twisted angrily. "You saw what happened in here, didn't you?"

Jeff turned away in anger. He wove through the crowd, his jaw tight as he moved toward the door. The Nasty Frenchman could only glimpse the truth, but someone else saw more, much more. Somehow, Jeff knew that this past hour held the key to the whole problem, if he could only see it. Here was the answer to the whole tangled puzzle of the girl and Paul Conroe, of Dr. Schiml and the Mercy Men.

And he knew that when he reached the room, the girl would be waiting. She would be waiting with cold fire in her eyes, as she sat at the table, a small pair of colored dice lying before her in the dim light.

Jeff hurried down the darkened corridor, fear exploding in his brain. She would be there and he knew why she would be smoldering when he walked into the room. He had seen her eyes, seen her face as they had thrown the dice. He knew beyond any shadow of doubt who had been controlling the dice.

The girl was waiting, just as he had known she would. He stepped into the room and closed the door gently behind him, facing her desperate eyes as she rolled the colored dice back and forth in front of her. "Game," she challenged, her voice harsh and metallic.

The room was tense with silent fear as he sank down opposite her at the table.

CHAPTER SIX

Jeff reached out and took the dice from the girl's hand. "Put them away, Blackie," he said softly, "You don't have to prove anything. I know—"

"Game," she repeated harshly, shaking her head.

"Look. Think a minute. Back there, do you know what happened in that room?"

Her eyes caught his and were wide with fear. "Game," she whispered, her hands trembling. "You've got to play me!"

He shrugged, his eyes tired as he watched her face. He took the dice and rolled them out on the table. A three, a four and a five fell; he saw her eyes flash across the table, taking in the sequence. Then her hand reached out, grasped the dice, gave them a throw. The hostility in her mind struck out at him, reinforcing the terrible dread that he already felt. He fought the hostility, staring at the dice, his hands gripping the edge of the table. And the dice danced and settled down: a three, a four and a five....

The girl's eyes widened, staring first at him, then back at the dice. Slowly she reached out, took the cube with the five showing, sent it bouncing across the table. It spun and bounced—and settled down once again with the five exposed.

Jeff felt the blast of bitter fear strike out from the girl's eyes. The room seemed to scream with the tension he felt. She took the dice with trembling hands, threw them out hard and clenched her fists as they fell. The three and four settled out immediately. Jeff watched the third cube, spinning on one corner, spinning ... spinning.... He felt his muscles grow tense, his mind screaming, tightening down as he stared at the little cube. It was as though an iron fist held his brain in its palm and was slowly, slowly squeezing. And the little cube continued, ridiculously, to spin and spin, until it quite suddenly flipped over onto its side and lay still with the five exposed.

Blackie gave a choked scream, her face pasty white. "Then it was you." She choked, staring at him as if he were a ghost. "You were doing it deliberately in there, throwing off the odds, twisting things around, turning the dice against me."

Jeff shook his head violently. "No, no, not me—us—both of us. We were fighting each other, without knowing it—"

48

Her hand went up to her mouth, choking off the words as she stared at him. Jeff stared at the dice, his whole body trembling, huge drops of sweat running down his forehead. And as he watched, the dice hopped about on the table, like jumping beans, turning over and over, jerkily, spinning on their edges in a horrible, incredible little dance. Jeff shook his head, his eyes wide with horror as he watched the dice.

"You knew it all along," the girl choked. "You came in there just to torment me, to show me up—"

"No, no." Jeff turned wide eyes on her. "I didn't know it, until I picked up the dice in that room. Something drove me to do it. I didn't know what I was doing until all of a sudden the dice were doing what I wanted them to do—" He broke off, panting. "I never knew it, I never dreamed it." His eyes sought the girl's, pleading. "I didn't understand it; I couldn't help it. I just knew that something wrong was going on. And then I knew that somebody was fighting me. There was a tension in it. I felt it. I knew somebody was tampering with the dice. Then when I got near you, I knew it was you."

The girl's face was working, tears welling up in her eyes. "I had to—I had to win with them."

"Then you knew you were doing it!" Jeff stared at her. "And when both of us started tampering, opposing each other, the probabilities governing the games went wild, completely wild."

The girl was sobbing, her face in her hands. "I could always control it. It always worked. It was the only thing I could do that came out right. Everything else has always gone wrong." She sobbed like a baby, her shoulders shaking as she choked out great, racking sobs.

Jeff leaned forward, almost cruelly, his eyes burning at her. "When did you find out you could ... make dice fall the way you wanted them to?"

The girl shook her head helplessly. "I didn't know it. I didn't have any idea, until I came here. It was the only thing I could win at. Everything else I lost at. All my life I've been losing."

"What have you been losing?"

"Everything, everything—everything I touch turns black, goes sour, somehow."

"But what, *what?*" Jeff leaned toward the girl, his voice hoarse. "Why did you come here? How did you get here?"

49

The girl's sobs broke out again, her shoulders shaking in anguish. "I don't know, I don't know. Oh, I could take it, up to a limit, but then I couldn't stand it any more. Everything I tried went wrong; everyone that was near me went wrong too. Even the rackets wouldn't work with me around."

"What rackets?"

Her voice was weak and cracking. "Any of the rackets. I've been in a dozen, two dozen, ever since the war. Dad was killed in the first bombing of the Fourth War, when I was just a kid—twelve, thirteen, I can't remember now. He died trying to get us out of the city and through to the Defense area north of the Trenton section. Radiation burns got him, maybe pneumonia, I don't know. But it got Dad first and Mom later."

She straightened up and wiped her eyes with her sleeve. "We never did get out of the devastated area. We were killing dogs and cats for food for a while. Then when things did get straightened out, we ran into the inflation, the burned-out crops, the whole rat-race. The dirty breaks were coming in hard then. First we were guerrillas, then we were bushwhackers. Then we came into the city again and started shaking down the rich ones that came back from the mountains where they hid."

"But you came in here," Jeff grated. "Why here, if you were doing so well in rackets?"

"I wasn't. Can't you understand? The luck—it was running wrong, worse and worse all the time. And then I got hooked on dope. Narcotics control was all shot to pieces during the war; heroin was all over the place. But they knew I had this hard-luck jinx. They caught me on it, until I was hooked bad."

She shrugged, her face a study in pathetic hopelessness. "They hauled me in here. Schiml sold me his bill of goods. What could I lose? I was so tired, I didn't care. I didn't care if they jolted my brains loose, or what they did to me. All I wanted was to eat and get off the dope and get enough cash so I could try for something decent, where hard luck couldn't touch me. And I didn't really care if I never got out."

"But with the dice you made out."

"Oh, yes, with the dice—" The girl's eyes flickered for a moment. "I found out I could make them sit up and talk for me. I played it cozy, didn't let anybody catch on. But they always worked for me, until tonight—"

Jeff nodded, his face white. "Until tonight, when you found out you were fighting for control. Because tonight I found out they'd talk for me too. And you couldn't beat me with them."

Her voice was weak. "I—I couldn't budge them. They fell the way you called them."

"It isn't possible, you know," Jeff said softly. "Every time they've tried to prove it was, they've found some loophole in the study of it, something wrong somewhere. Nobody's ever proved a thing about psychokinesis."

The girl grinned mirthlessly. "They've been trying to prove it here since the year one. Every now and again they get hot on it. They've just tested somebody that's got them excited and they'll be starting the whole works over again."

Jeff leaned over, his eyes blazing. "Yes, yes, who's that person?"

"I don't know. I just heard it. A new recruit, I guess."

"A recruit named Conroe?"

Her eyes widened at the virulence in his voice. "I—I don't know, I don't know. I've only heard. I don't even know if there *is* such a person."

"Where can I find out?"

Again the fear was in her eyes. "I—I don't know."

Jeff's voice was tense, his eyes fixed on the girl's face in desperate eagerness. "Look, you've got to help me. I know he's here. I must find him. I saw him this afternoon. Remember when the guards brought me in here? I saw him on the stairs. I chased him and lost him, but he's here. He's hiding, running away from me. I've got to find him, somehow. Please, Blackie, you can help me."

Her eyes were wide on his face. "What do you want with him? Why are you after him? I don't want to get mixed up in anything—"

"No, no, it won't mix you up. Look, I want to kill him. Short and sweet, nothing more—just kill him. I want to send one bullet into his brain, watch his face splatter out, watch his skull break open. That's all I want, just one bullet—"

Jeff's voice was low, the words wrenched from his throat, and the hatred in his eyes was poisonous as it washed over the girl's face. "He haunts me, for years he's haunted me." Jeff's voice dropped, the words breaking the stillness of the room in a hoarse, terrible cadence. "He killed my father. This Conroe—he butchered my father like an animal, shot him down in cold blood. It was horrible, ruthless. Conroe was the assassin. He killed my father without a thought of mercy in his mind. And I loved my father, I loved him with all the love I had." He stared at the girl. "I'll kill the man that killed my father if I have to die myself in the killing."

"And that man is here?"

"That man is here. I've hunted him for years. This was his last resort, his final desperate gamble for escape. He had nowhere else to turn. I've got the outside tied up so that he doesn't dare to leave. Now I've got to track him down in here. I've got to find him and kill him, before I'm caught, before I'm tested and classified. I've got to move fast and I need help. I need help so much."

The girl leaned toward him, her eyes dark as she stared at him. "The dice," she said softly. "I've been playing it cozy. I still could—if you'll let me."

His eyes widened. "Anything you say," he said. "We'll play it cozy together. But I've got to have floor plans of the place, information on how to avoid the guards. I've got to know where their records are kept, their lists and rosters and working plans."

"Then it's a deal?"

His eyes caught hers, and for an instant he saw something behind the mask she wore, something of the fear that lay back there, something of a little child who fought against impossible odds to find a toehold in the world. Then the barrier was back up, and her eyes were blank and revealed nothing.

Jeff held out his hand, touched her palm lightly and clenched her fingers. "It's a deal," he said.

*

The trip down the corridor was a nightmare. Jeff's mind was still reeling from the incredible discovery of the dice, the sudden, unbelievable awareness that he and Blackie had been silently and fiercely battling each other for control, fighting with a fury that had somehow shattered the very warp of probability in the room where they had been. How could he have had a part in something like this? He had never had reason to suspect he might carry such a power, yet here was evidence he could not disregard. And how could it fit into the question of Paul Conroe, and the mysterious recruit to the Mercy Men who had just been tested?

ALAN E. NOURSE

A thought struck Jeff, quite suddenly. It came with such impact that he stopped cold in his tracks. It was so simple, so impossible, yet no more impossible than the things he had already seen with his own eyes. Because the incredible record of escapes that Conroe carried, the impossible regularity with which Conroe had managed to avoid capture, time after time, seemed too much to accept as coincidence. And if Conroe were indeed carrying latent extra-sensory powers, he could continue to slip from trap after trap—*unless Jeff could oppose those powers with powers of his own.*

Jeff cursed in his teeth. How could he tell? He had no evidence that Conroe carried any extra-sensory power whatsoever, and surely there was little enough to indicate that he had any more than most latent powers. There were so many, many possibilities, and so little concrete evidence to go on.

And if Conroe had such powers, why had he been so startled to meet Jeff on the stairs? Why the look of fear and disbelief that had streaked across his face? Jeff glanced at his watch, saw the minute hand move to eleven-thirty. He would have to hurry, for the guards would be down the escalator in a few moments. And these thoughts of his could lead to nowhere. Conroe had been jolted to see Jeff. It must have been a horrible shock for him to realize that the Hunter had followed him, even into this death trap, to know that the Hunter would have the outside so well guarded that he, the Hunted, could never get out. Now Conroe would be forced to gamble against being caught and assigned to work as a Mercy Man. Yes, it must have been a horrible jolt for Conroe, driving one last, searing bolt of fear into his already desperate mind. And what would he have tried to do?

A thousand ideas flooded Jeff's mind. He was waiting for testing. Perhaps Conroe, somehow, had been tested already? Could Jeff succeed in stalling Schiml, especially if the rumors spinning down the dark corridors were true? There was no sure way of telling. All Jeff could do was to search the file rooms Blackie had directed him to.

He stopped at the entrance to the escalator, pored over the floor plan Blackie had sketched for him. He spotted the escalator, oriented himself on the plan. The filing rooms were two flights below. If he could reach them without being stopped.... He moved silently onto the down shaft, his eyes moving constantly for a sight of a gray-garbed prowler.

A MAN OBSESSED

At the foot of the escalator he stopped short. Three men in white were pushing a gurney along the corridor. Jeff glanced quickly at the twitching form under the blankets. Then he looked away hurriedly. One of the men dropped behind and waved at him sharply as he stepped off the stairs. The man still wore the operating mask hanging from his neck, and his hair was tightly enclosed in the green-knit operating cap.

The doctor tipped a thumb over his shoulder and pointed down the corridor. "You coming to fix the pump?"

Jeff blinked rapidly. "That's right," he croaked. "Did—did Jerry come with the tools yet?"

"Nobody came in yet. We just finished. Been in there since three this afternoon, and the damned pump went kerflooey right in the middle. Had to aspirate the poor joe by hand, and if you think *that's* not a job—" The doctor wiped sweat from his forehead. "Better get it fixed tonight. We've got another one going in at eight in the morning and we've got to have the pump."

Jeff nodded, and started down the hall, his heart thudding madly against his ribs. He reached the open door to one of the operating rooms. Slipping quickly into the small dressing-room annex, he snatched one of the gowns and caps from the wall.

If they were still operating this late, it was a heaven-sent chance. No guard would bother him if he were wearing the white of a doctor or the green of a surgeon. He struggled into the clumsy gowning, tying it quickly behind his back, and slipped the cap over his head. Finally he found a mask, snapped it up under his ears as he had seen it worn by the doctors in the corridors.

In a moment he was back on the escalator, descending to the next floor. At the foot of the stairs, he started quickly down the corridor Blackie had indicated, glancing at each door as he passed. The first two had lights under them, indicating that these apparently were operating rooms still in use. Finally he stopped before a large, heavy door, with a simple sign painted on the wooden panel: COMPUTER TECHNICIANS ONLY. He tried the door, found it locked. Quickly he glanced up and down the corridor, doubled a hard fist and drove it through the panel with a crunch. Then he fumbled inside for the lock.

In an instant he was inside. The torn hole in the panel glared at him. He threw the door wide open and snapped on the overhead lights, throwing the room into bright fluorescent light. Then he drew the pale-green gown closer about him and moved across the room to the huge file panel that faced him.

It was not his first experience with the huge punched-card files which had become so necessary in organizations where the numbers and volumes of records made human operatives too slow or clumsy. Quickly Jeff moved to the master-control panel, searched for the section and coding system for Research: Subject Personnel.

First he would try the simple coding for Conroe's name, on the chance that Conroe had come in using his own name. Jeff rechecked the coding, punched the buttons which would relay through the cards alphabetically; then he waited as the machinery whirred briefly. A panel lighted near the bottom of the control board, spelling the two words: NO INFORMATION.

Jeff's fingers sped over the coding board again, as he started coding in a description. He coded in height, weight, eye color, hair color, bone contour, lip formation—every other descriptive category he could think of. Then again he punched the "Search" button.

This time several dozen cards fell down. He picked them up from the yield-slot and slowly leafed through them, glancing both at the small photograph attached to each card and at the small "date of admission" code symbol at the top of each card. Again he found nothing. Disgusted, he tried the same system again, this time adding two limiting coding symbols: Subject Personnel and Recent Admission. And again the cards were negative. Not a single one could possibly have been connected with Paul Conroe.

Jeff sat down at the desk facing the panel and he searched his mind for another pathway of identification. Suddenly a thought occurred to him. He searched through his pocket for a picture wallet, drew out the small, ID-size photo of Conroe that he carried for identification purposes.

Searching the panel, he finally found the slot he was looking for: the small, photoelectronic chamber for recording picture identification. He slipped the photo into the slot, punched the "Search" button, and waited again, his whole body tense.

A MAN OBSESSED

The machine buzzed for a long moment. Then a single card dropped into the slot. Eagerly Jeff snatched it up, stared down at the attached photograph which almost perfectly matched the photo from his pocket. Near the top of the card was a small typewritten notation: *Conroe, Paul A.*, INFORMATION RESTRICTED. ALL FILE NOTATIONS RECORDED IN HOFFMAN CENTER CENTRAL ARCHIVES.

Below this notation was a list of dates. Jeff read them, staring in disbelief, then read them again. Incredible, those dates—dates of admission to the Hoffman Center and dates of release. It was impossible that Conroe could have been here at the times the dates indicated: ten years ago, when the Hoffman Center was hardly opened; five years ago, during the very time when Jeff had been tracking him down. Yet the dates were there, in black and white, cold, impersonal, indisputable. And below the dates was a final notation, inked in by hand: CENTRAL ARCHIVES CLASSIFICATION: ESP RESEARCH.

Swiftly Jeff stuffed the card into his shirt. He refiled the other cards with trembling fingers, his heart pounding a frightful tattoo in his forehead. Incredible, yet he knew, somehow, that it fit into the picture, that it was a key to the picture. He turned, started for the door, and stopped dead.

"Schiml!" he breathed.

The figure lounged against the door, green cap askew on his head, mask still dangling about his neck. There was a smile on his face as he leaned back, regarding Jeff in amusement. Nonchalantly, he tossed a pair of dice into the air, and caught them, still smiling. "Let's go, Jeff," said Dr. Schiml. "We've got some tests to run."

"You—you mean, in the morning," Jeff stammered, hardly believing his ears.

The smile broadened on the doctor's lips, and he gave the dice another toss and dropped them in his pocket. "Not in the morning, Jeff," he said softly. "Now."

56

CHAPTER SEVEN

Jeff sank down in the chair, his forehead streaming sweat. He clenched his fists as he tried to regain control of his trembling muscles. *How long had Schiml been standing there? Just a second or two?* Or had he been watching Jeff for ten minutes, watching him punch down the filing codes, watching him stuff the filing card into his shirt? There was nothing to be told from the doctor's face, as the man smiled down at his trembling quarry. There was nothing in the eyes of the guards who stood behind him in the hallway, their hands poised on their heavy sidearms.

Schiml turned to one of them, nodded slightly, and they disappeared, their boots clanging in the still corridor behind them. Then he turned his eyes back to Jeff, the ghost of a knowing smile still flickering about his eyes. "Find anything interesting?" he asked, his eyes narrowing slightly.

Jeff fumbled a cigarette to his lips, gripped the lighter to steady it. "Nothing to speak of," he said hoarsely. "Been a long time since I worked one of these files." His eyes caught Schiml's defiantly, held them in desperation. Finally Schiml blinked and looked away.

"Looking for anything special?" he asked smoothly.

"Nothing special." Jeff blew smoke out into the room, his trembling nerves quieting slightly.

"I see. Just sight-seeing, I suppose."

Jeff shrugged. "More or less. I wanted to see the setup."

A dry smile crossed Schiml's face. "Particularly the setup in the filing room," he said softly. "I thought I'd find you here. Blackie said you'd just stepped out for a short walk, so we just took a guess." The doctor's eyes hardened sharply on Jeff's face. "And all dressed up like a doctor, too."

He stepped across the room, jerked the cap from Jeff's head, snapped the string to the gown with a sharp swipe of his hand. "We don't do this around here," he said, his voice cutting like a razor. "Doctors wear these, nobody else. Got that straight? We also do not wander around breaking into filing rooms, just looking at the setup. If the guards had caught you at it, you wouldn't be alive right now—which would have been a dirty shame, since we have plans for you." He jerked his thumb toward the door. "After you, Jeff. We've got some work to do tonight."

Jeff moved out into the hall, took up beside the tall doctor as he started back for the escalator. "You weren't serious about testing me tonight, surely."

Dr. Schiml stared at him. "And why not?"

"Look, it's late. I'll be here in the morning."

The doctor walked on in silence for a long moment. Jeff followed, his mind racing, a thousand questions tumbling through in rapid succession: questions he dared not ask, questions he couldn't answer. How much did Schiml know? And how much did he suspect? A chill ran down Jeff's back. What had he been doing with the dice? Could Blackie possibly have told him? Or could he have heard about the freakish occurrence in the game room through other channels? And what could he learn in the course of the testing that he didn't know already?

Jeff puzzled as he matched the doctor's rapid pace. They went up the escalator, down the twisting corridor toward an area beyond the living quarters that Jeff hadn't seen before. Above all, he must keep his nerve, keep a tight control on his tongue, on his reactions, make sure that there were no tricks to tear information from him that he didn't dare divulge.

He looked at Schiml, sharply, a frown on his face. "I still don't see why this can't wait till morning. Why the big hurry?"

Schiml stopped, turned to Jeff in exasperation. "You still think we're running a picnic grounds here, don't you?" he snapped. "Well, we're not. We're doing a job, a job that can't wait for morning or anything else. We work a twenty-four-hour schedule here. All you do is provide the where-withal to work with—nothing more."

"But I'll be tired, nervous. I don't see how I could pass any kind of test."

Schiml laughed shortly. "These aren't the kind of tests you pass or fail. Actually, the more tired and nervous you are, the better the results will be for you. They'll give you an extra edge of safety when you're assigned to a job. What the tests tell us is what we can expect from you, the very minimum. Basically, we're working to save your life for you."

Jeff blinked at him, followed him through swinging doors into a long, brightly lighted corridor, with green walls and a gleaming tile floor. "What do you mean, save my life? You seem to delight in just the opposite here, from what I've heard."

The doctor made an impatient noise. "You got the wrong information," he said angrily. "That's the trouble. You people insist upon listening to and believing the morbid stories, all the unpleasantness you hear about the work here. And it's all either completely false or only half-truth. This business of bloodthirstiness, for instance. It's just plain not true.

"One of the biggest factors in our work here is making arrangements for optimum conditions for the success of our experiments. By 'optimum' we mean the best conditions from several standpoints: from the standpoint of what we're trying to learn—the experiment itself, that is—and from the standpoint of the researcher, too. But most particularly, we're working for optimum recovery odds for the experimental animals—you, in this case."

Jeff snorted. "But still, we're just experimental animals, from your viewpoint," he said sharply.

"Not *just* experimental animals," Schiml snapped angrily. "You're *the* experimental animals. Working with human beings isn't the same as working with cats and dogs and monkeys—far from it. Dogs and cats are stronger and tougher, more durable than humans, which is why they're used for preliminary work of great success. But basically, they're expendable. If something goes wrong, that's too bad. But we've learned something, and the dog or cat can be sacrificed without too many tears. But we don't feel quite the same about human beings."

"I'm glad to hear that," said Jeff sourly. "It makes me feel better."

"I'm not trying to be facetious. I mean it. We're not ghouls. We don't have any less regard for human life than anyone else, just because we're responsible for some human death in the work we're doing. For one thing, we study every human being we use, try to dig out his strengths and weaknesses, physical and mental. We want to know how he reacts to what, how fast he recuperates, how much physical punishment his body can take, how far his mental resiliency will extend. Then when we know these things, we can fit him into the program of research which will give him the very best chance of coming out in one piece. At the same time, he will fill a spot that we need filled. No, there's no delight here in taking human life or jeopardizing human safety."

They turned abruptly off the corridor and entered a small office. Schiml motioned Jeff to a chair, sat himself down behind a small desk and began sorting through several stacks of forms. The room was silent for a moment. Then the doctor punched a button on the telephone panel.

When the light blinked an answer to him, he said: "Gabe? He's here. Better come on up."

Then he flipped down the switch and leaned back, lighting a long, slender cigar and undoing the green robe around his neck.

Jeff watched him, still puzzling over what he had just said. The doctor seemed so matter-of-fact. What he had said made sense, but somewhere in the picture there seemed to be a gaping hole. "This sounds like it's a great setup—for you doctors and researchers," he said finally. "But what's it leading to? What good is it doing? Oh, I know, it increases your knowledge of men's minds, but how does it help the man in the street? How does it actually help *anyone*, in the long run? How do you ever get the government to back it with the financial mess they're facing in Washington?"

Schiml threw back his head and laughed aloud. "You've got the cart before the horse," he said, when he got control of his voice. "Support? Listen, my lad, the government is running itself bankrupt just to keep our research going. Did you realize that? *Bankrupting itself!* And why? Because unless our work pays off—and soon—there isn't going to be any government left. That's why. Because we're fighting something that's eating away at the very roots of our civilization, something that's creeping and growing and destroying."

He stared at Jeff, his eyes wide. "Oh, the government knows that the situation is grave. We had to prove it to them, show it to them time and again, until they couldn't miss it any longer. But they saw it finally. They've seen it growing for a century or more, ever since the end of the Second War. They've seen the business instability, the bank runs and the stock market dives. They've seen the mental and moral decay in the cities. They could see it, but it took statistics to prove that there was a pattern to it, a pattern of decay and rot and putrefaction that's been crumbling away the clay feet of this colossal civilization of ours."

The doctor stood up, paced back and forth across the room and sent blue smoke into the air from the cigar as he walked. "Oh, they support us all right. We don't know for sure what we're fighting, but we do know the answer is in the functioning of the minds and brains of man. We're working against a disease—a creeping disease of men's minds—and we are forced to use men to search those minds, to study them, to try to weed out the poison of the disease. And so we have the Mercy Men to help us fight."

The doctor's lips twisted in a bitter sneer as he sat heavily down on the chair again, crunched the cigar out viciously in the tray. "Mercy Men who have no mercy in their souls, who have no interest nor concern with what they're doing, or what it may be accomplishing. They are interested in one thing only: the amount of money they'll be paid for having their brains jogged loose."

The scorn was heavy in Dr. Schiml's eyes. "Well, we don't care who we have: addicts, condemned murderers, prostitutes, the trash from the skid-row gutters. They're all drawn here, like flies to a dung hill. But they're here on errands of mercy, whether they like it or not, or know it or not. And we take them because they're the only ones who can be bought, and we guard them for all we're worth, so that the goal will be accomplished." He took a deep breath and stared scornfully at Jeff. "That's you I'm talking about, you know."

Jeff's hands trembled as he snuffed out his smoke. He stood up as the corridor door opened, admitting a small, dark-haired man with thick glasses. He was dressed in doctor's whites. Jeff rubbed his chest nervously and took a deep breath, still acutely aware of the stiff card in his shirt front.

"All right," he said hoarsely, "so you're talking about me. When do we get started with this?"

*

The little dressing room was cramped; it reeked of anesthetic. Jeff walked in, followed by Dr. Schiml and the other doctor, and started removing his shoes. "This is Doctor Gabriel," Schiml said, indicating his myopic colleague. "He'll start you off with a complete physical. Then you'll have a neurological. Come on into the next room as soon as you're undressed." And with that the two doctors disappeared through swinging doors into an inner room.

Jeff removed his shirt and trousers swiftly, carefully folding the file card and stuffing it under the inner sole of his right shoe. It wasn't exactly the perfect hiding place, if anyone were looking for the card. But not once during the conversation had Schiml's eyes strayed curiously to Jeff's shirt front. Either Schiml had not seen him take the card, or else the doctor's self-control was superhuman. And no mention of the dice had been made, either. Jeff gave his shoes a final pat, tossed his clothes on one of the gurneys lining the walls and pushed through the doors into the next room.

It was huge, dome-ceilinged, with a dozen partitions dividing different sections from one another. One end looked like a classroom, with blackboards occupying a whole wall. Another section carried the paraphernalia of a complete gymnasium. The doctors were sitting in a corner that was obviously outfitted as an examination room: the tables were covered with crisp green sheeting, and the walls had gleaming cabinets full of green-wrapped bundles and instruments.

Schiml sat on the edge of a desk. His eyes watched Jeff closely as he lit a cigarette, leaned back and blew rings into the air. Dr. Gabriel motioned Jeff to the table and started the physical without further delay.

It was the most rigorous, painstaking physical examination Jeff had ever had. The little, squinting doctor poked and probed him from head to toe. He snapped retinal-pattern photos, examined pore-patterns, listened, prodded, thumped, auscultated. He motioned Jeff back onto the chair and started going over him with a rubber hammer, tapping him sharply in dozens of areas, eliciting a most disconcerting variety of muscular jerks and twitches. Then the hammer was replaced by a small electrode, with which the doctor probed and tested, bringing spasmodic jerks to the muscles of Jeff's back and arms and thighs. Finally, Dr. Gabriel relaxed, sat Jeff down in a soft chair and retired to a small portable instrument cabinet nearby.

Dr. Schiml put out his smoke and stood up. "Any questions before we begin?"

Jeff almost sighed aloud. Any questions? His nerves tingled all over and his mind was full of conjecture—wild, ridiculous guesses of what they would discover in the testing, of what the results would bring. Suppose they learned about the dice? Suppose they found out that he was a fraud, that he was in the Center on a private mission, a mission of death all his own, and no party to their own missions of death? And yet, if he had to follow through, the kind of work he would be assigned to would depend upon the results of the tests—that seemed sure. But what if they rendered him unconscious, knocked him out, used drugs?

His mind raced frantically, searching for some way of stalling things, some way of slowing down the red tape of testing and assignment, to give him time to complete his own mission and get out. But he knew that already he must have aroused suspicions. Schiml must have suspected that all the cards were not on the table, yet Schiml seemed willing to overlook his suspicions. And the wheels had begun to move more and more swiftly, carrying him to the critical point where he would have to sign a release and take an assignment, or reveal his real purpose for being in the Center. If he were to find Conroe, he must find him before the chips were down.

He stared at Schiml, his mind still groping for something to hang onto. He found nothing. "No. No questions, I guess," he said.

The doctor looked at him closely, then shrugged in resignation. "All right," he said, tiredly. "You'll have a whole series of tests of all kinds: physical stamina, mental alertness, reaction time, intelligence, sanity—everything we could possibly need to know. But I should warn you of one thing." He looked at Jeff, his eyes deadly serious. "All of these future tests are subjective. All of them will tell us about you as a person: how you think, how you behave. Desperately essential stuff, if you're to survive the sort of work we do here. What we find is the whole basis of our assignments."

He paused for a long moment. "You'd be wise to stick to the truth. No embellishments, no fancy stuff. We can't do anything about it if you don't choose to take the advice. But if you falsify, you're tampering with your own life expectancy here."

Jeff blinked, shifting in his seat uneasily. *Don't worry about that, Jack*, he thought. *I won't be around long enough for it to make any difference.* Nevertheless the doctor's words were far from soothing. If only Jeff could maintain the fraud throughout the testing, keep his wits about him as the tests progressed. Then he could get back to the hunt as soon as they were through.

He watched the doctor prepare a long paper on the desk. Then the rapid-fire series of questions began: family history, personal history, history of family disease and personal illness. The questions were swift and businesslike, and Jeff felt his muscles relaxing as he sat back. He answered almost automatically. Then: "Ever been hypnotized before?"

Something in Jeff's mind froze, screaming a warning. "No," he snapped.

Schiml's eyes widened imperceptibly. "Part of the testing should be done under hypnosis, for your sake, and for the sake of speed." His eyes caught Jeff's hard. "Unless you have some reason for objecting—"

"It won't work," Jeff lied swiftly, his mind racing. "Psychic block of some kind—induced in childhood, probably. My father had a block against it too." Every muscle in his body was tense, and he sat forward in his seat, his eyes wide.

Schiml shrugged. "It would make the testing a hundred per cent easier on you if you'd allow it. Some of these tests are pretty exhausting and some take a powerful long time without hypnotic-recovery aid. And of course we keep all information strictly confidential—"

"No dice," said Jeff hoarsely.

The doctor shrugged again, glancing over at Dr. Gabriel. "Hear that, Gabe?"

The little doctor shrugged. "His funeral," he growled. He rolled a small, shiny-paneled instrument with earphones to Jeff's side. "We'll start on the less strenuous ones, then. This is a hearing test. Very simple. You just listen, mark down the signals you hear. Keep your eyes on the eyepiece; it records visio-audio correlation times, tells us how soon after you hear a word you form a visual image of it." He snapped the earphones over Jeff's head and moved a printed answer sheet in front of him on the desk. And then the earphones started talking.

There was a long series of words, gradually becoming softer and softer. Jeff marked them down, swiftly, gradually forgetting his surroundings, throwing his attention toward the test. The doctors retired to the other side of the room. They talked to each other in low whispers, until he no longer heard them. There was only the low, insistent whispering in the earphones.

And then the words seemed to grow louder again, but somehow he had lost track of what they meant. He listened, his eyes watching the cool gray pearly screen in the eyepieces. His fingers were poised to write down the words, but he couldn't quite understand the syllables.

They were *nonsense syllables*, syllables with no meaning. His eyes opened wide, a bolt of suspicion shooting through him, and his hands gripped the arms of the chair as he began to rise.

And then the light exploded in his eyes with such agonizing brilliance that it sent shooting pain searing through his brain. He let out a stifled cry. He struggled and tried to rise from the chair. But he was blinded by the piercing beam. And then he felt the needle bite his arm, and the nonsense words in his ears straightened out into meaningful phrases. A soft, soothing voice was saying: "Relax ... relax ... sit back and relax ... relax and rest...."

Slowly the warmth crept over his body, and he felt his muscles relax, even as the voice instructed. He eased gently back into the chair, and soon his mind was clear of fear and worry and suspicion. He was still, sleeping with the peaceful ease of a newborn child.

CHAPTER EIGHT

It could never have been done without hypnosis. Within broad limits, the human body is capable of doing just exactly whatever it *thinks* it is capable of. But the human body could hardly be blamed if convention had long since decided that exertion was bad, that straining to the limit of endurance was unhealthy, that approaching—even obliquely—the margin of safety of human resiliency was equivalent to approaching death with arms extended. That convention had so declared was well known to the researchers at the Hoffman Center.

But it was also known that the human body under the soothing suggestion of hypnosis could be carried up to that margin of safety and beyond. Indeed, it could be carried almost to the actual breaking point without stir, without a flicker of protest, without a sign of fear.

And these were the conditions that were critically needed in testing for the Mercy Men. Yet, though hypnosis was necessary, the men who came to the Mercy Men without fail rejected hypnosis. Always they held the fear of divulging some secret of their past. Whether because of distrust of the doctors and the testing in the Center, or plain, ordinary malignance of character—no one knew all the motives. But those who needed hypnosis the most rejected it the most vehemently. This forced the development of techniques of hypnosis-by-force.

It would have annoyed Jeff, if he had known. Indeed, it would have driven him to the heights of anger, for Jeff, among other things, was afraid. But he need not have been, and it made little difference that he was. Now Jeff was not suffering from his fear. His mind was in a quiet, happy haze, and he felt his body half-lifted, half-led across the room to the first section of the testing room.

Even now there was a tiny, sharp-voiced sentinel hiding away in a corner of his mind, screaming out its message of alertness and fear to Jeff. But he laughed to himself, sinking deeper into the peacefulness of his walking slumber. Dr. Gabriel's voice was in his ear, his voice smooth and soothing, talking to him quietly, giving simple instructions. Quickly, he took him through the paces of a testing series that would have taken long, hard days to complete. It would have left him in psychotic break at the end, if he had not had the recuperative buffer of hypnosis to help him.

First, he was dressed in soft flannel clothing and moved into the gymnasium. Recorders were attached to his legs and arms and throat. Then he was formally introduced to the treadmill and quietly asked to run it until he collapsed. He smiled and obliged, running as though the furies were at his heels. He ran until his face went purple and his muscles knotted. At last he fell down, unable to continue.

This happened after ten minutes of top-limit running. Then came five minutes of recuperation under suggestion: "Your heart is beating slower. You're breathing slowly and deeply ... relaxing ... relaxing." Someone took his arm and he was off again, this time on the old, reliable Harvard Step-Test, jumping up on the chair and back down. He did this until once again he lay panting on the floor, hardly able to move as his pulse and respiration changes were carefully recorded.

Next in line came a lively handball game. He was handed a small, hard-rubber ball, and asked to engage in a game of catch with a machine that was stationed at the end of a cubby. The machine played hard, spinning the ball around and hurling it at Jeff with such incredible rapidity that he was forced to abandon all thinking. Instinctively, he reached out to catch the ball. His fingers burned with pain as he caught it and passed it in, only to have it hurled back out again, twice as fast. Soon he moved as automatically as a machine, catching, hurling, his mind refusing to accept the aching and swelling in his fingers, as the ball struck and struck and struck....

Then a small ladder was rolled in. He listened carefully to instructions and then ran up and down the ladder until he collapsed off the top. He was rested gently on the floor while blood samples were taken from his arm. Then he sat, staring dully at the floor. A voice said, "Relax, Jeff, take a rest. Sleep quietly, Jeff. You'll be ready to dig in and fight in a minute. Now just relax."

Several people were about; one brought him a heavy, sugary drink, lukewarm and revolting. He drank it, gagging, spilling it all down his shirt front. Then he grinned and licked his lips while further blood samples were drawn. And then, he was allowed to take a drink of cool water. He was left staring at his feet for five whole minutes of recuperation before the next stage of the testing commenced.

*

A MAN OBSESSED

The lights were in three long columns. They extended as far as Jeff could see to the horizon. Some were blinking; some shone with steady intensity, while others were dark.

"Call the columns one, two and three," said Dr. Gabriel, close by, his voice soft with patience. "Record the position of the lights as you see them now. Then when the signal sounds, start recording every light change you see in all three columns. Do it fast, Jeff, as fast as you can."

The eye is a wonderful instrument of precision, capable of detecting an infinitude of movement and change. It is delicate enough to distinguish, if necessary, each and every still frame composing the motion picture that flickers so swiftly before it on the white screen. Jeff's fingers moved, his pencil recorded, quickly moving from column one to column two, and on to column three. The pencil moved swiftly until the test was over.

Then on to the next test....

Electrode leads were fastened to each of his ten toes and each of his ten fingers.

"Listen once, Jeff. Right first toe corresponds to left thumb; right second toe to right index finger. (Wonderful stuff, hypno-palamine, only one repetition to learn) When you feel a shock in a toe, press the button for the corresponding finger. Ready now, Jeff, as fast as you can."

Shock, press, shock, press. Jeff's mind was still, silent, a blank, an open circuit for reactions to speed through without hindrance, without modulation. Another round done and on to the next....

Doctor Schiml's pale face loomed up from some distant place. "Everything all right?"

"Going fine, fine. Smooth as can be."

"No snags anywhere?"

"No, no snags. None that I can see—yet."

*

"I want a smoke."

Dr. Gabriel relaxed, offered Jeff a smoke from a crumpled pack, extended his lighter and smiled. He noticed that Jeff's wide eyes missed their focus, could not see the extended flame. "How do you feel, Jeff?"

"Fine, fine—"

"Still got a lot to do."

A flicker of fear crossed the dull eyes. "Fine. Only I hope...."

"Yes?"

"... hope we finish. I'm tired."

"Sleepy?"

"Yeah, sleepy."

"Well, we'll have everything on punched cards for Tilly in a couple of hours or so. All the factors about you that this testing will unearth would take a research staff five hundred years to integrate down to the point where it would mean anything. With Tilly it takes five minutes. She doesn't make mistakes, either."

"Nice Tilly."

"And after the results come through, you're assigned and you sign your release and you're on your way to money."

Again the flicker of fear came, deeper this time. "Money...."

*

More tests, more tests. Hear a sound, punch a button. See a picture, record it. Test after endless test, dozens of records, his brain growing tired, tired. Then into the bright, gleaming room, up onto the green-draped table.

"No pain, Jeff, nothing to worry about. Be over in just a minute."

His eyes caught the slender, wicked-looking trefine; he heard the buzz of the motor, felt the grinding shock. But there was no reaction, no pain. And then he felt a curious tingling in his arms and legs, as the small electro-encephalograph end-plates entered his skull through the tiny drilled holes.

He watched with dull eyes as the little lights on the control board nearby began blinking on and off, on and off. The flashes followed a hectic, nervous pattern, registering individual brain-cell activity onto supersensitive stroboscopic film. This, in turn, was fed down automatically to Tilly for analysis. And then the trefine holes were plugged up again and his head was tightly taped, and he was moved back into another room for another five-minute recovery.

"Hit the ink blots yet?"

"Not yet, Rog. Take it easy, we're coming along. Ink blots and intelligence runs next, and so on."

Something stirred deep in Jeff's mind, even through the soothing delusions of hypnosis. It stirred and cried out at the first sign of the strange,

69

colored forms on the cards. Something deep in Jeff's mind forced its way out to his lips as Dr. Gabriel said softly, "Just look at them, Jeff, and tell me what you see."

"No! Take them away."

"What's that? Gently, Jeff. Relax and take a look."

Jeff was on his feet, backing away, a wild, helpless, cornered fire in his eyes. "Take them away. Get me out of here. Go away—"

"Jeff!" The voice was sharp, commanding. "Sit down, Jeff."

Jeff sank down in the seat, gingerly, eyes wary. The doctor moved his hand and Jeff jumped a foot, his teeth chattering.

"What's the matter, Jeff?"

"I—I don't like ... those ... cards."

"But they're only ink blots, Jeff."

Jeff frowned and squinted at the cards. He scratched his head in perplexity. Slowly he sank back down in the chair, didn't even notice as the web-belt restrainers closed over his arms and legs, tightened down.

"Now look at the pictures, Jeff. Tell me what you see."

The perplexity grew on his heavy face, but he looked and talked, slowly, hoarsely. A dog's head, a little gnome, a big red bat.

"Gently, Jeff. Nothing to be afraid of. Relax, man, relax...."

Then came the word-association tests: half an hour of words and answers, while fear curled up through Jeff's brain, gathering, crouching, ready to spring, waiting in horrible anticipation for something, something that was coming as sure as hour followed hour. Jeff felt the web restrainers cutting his wrists, as the words were read. He trembled in growing foreboding.

Dr. Schiml's face was back, still concerned, his eyes bright. "Going all right, Gabe?"

"Dunno, Rog. Something funny with the ink blots. You can glance at the report. Word association all screwed up too. Can't spot it, but there's something funny."

"Give him a minute's rest and reinforce the palamine. Probably got a powerful vitality opposing it."

Dr. Gabriel was back in a moment, and another needle nibbled Jeff's arm briefly. Then the doctor walked to the desk, took out the small, square plastic box. He dropped the cards out into his hand. They were plain-backed little cards with bright red symbols on their faces.

Dr. Gabriel held them under Jeff's nose. "Rhine cards," he said softly. "Four different symbols, Jeff. Look close. A square, a circle...."

It was like a gouge, jammed down through Jeff's mind, ripping it without mercy. A red-hot, steaming poker was being rammed into the soft, waxy tissue of his brain.

"My God, hold him!"

Jeff screamed, wide awake, his eyes bulging with terror. With an animal-like roar he wrenched at his restrainers, ripped them out of the raw wood and plunged across the room in blind, terrified flight. He ran across the room and struck the solid brick wall full face. He hit with a sickening thud, pounded at the wall with his fists, screaming out again and again. And then he collapsed to the floor, his nose broken, his face bleeding, his fingers raw with the nails broken.

And as he slid into merciful unconsciousness, they heard him blubbering: "He killed my father ... killed him ... killed him ... killed him ... killed him...."

*

Hours later he stirred. He almost screamed out in pain as he tried to move his arm. His chest burned as he breathed. When he opened his eyes, an almost unbearable, pounding ache struck down through his skull. He recognized his room, saw the empty bed across from him. Then he raised an arm, felt the bandaging around his face, his neck.

He listened fearfully and his ears caught only the harsh, gurgling breathing of the man in the next room: the man called Tinker, whose doom as a Mercy Man had not been quite sealed, who breathed on, shallowly, breaking the deadly silence.

What had happened?

Jeff sat bolt upright in the darkness, ignoring the stabbing pain that shot through his chest and neck. What had happened? Why was he bandaged? What was the meaning of the pure, naked, paralyzing fear that was gripping him like a vise? He stared through the darkness at the opposite bed, and blinked. What had happened ... what ... what?

Of course. He had been in the file room. He'd been caught. Schiml had caught him and he had been taken down for testing. And then: *a bright light, nonsense words in his ear, a needle....*

A MAN OBSESSED

Gasping with pain, Jeff rolled out of bed, searched underneath for his shoes. With an audible sob, he retrieved the crumpled card from under the inner sole. Then they hadn't gotten the card. They didn't know. But what could have happened? Slowly, other things came back: there had been a scream; he had felt a shock, as though molten lead had been sent streaming through his veins, and then he had struck the wall like a ten-ton truck.

He groped for his watch, stared at it, hardly believing his eyes. It read seven P.M. It had been almost one A.M. when they had taken him down to Dr. Gabriel. It couldn't be seven in the evening again. Unless he had slept around the clock. He listened to the watch; it was still running. Whatever had happened had thrown him, thrown him so hard that he had slept for almost twenty-four hours. And in the course of that time....

The horrible loss struck him suddenly, worming its way through to open realization. Twenty-four hours later—a day gone, a whole day for Conroe to use to move deeper into hiding. He sank back on the bed and groaned, despair heavy in his mind. A day gone, a precious day. Somewhere the man was in the Center. But to locate him now, after he had had such time—how could Jeff do it?

He felt a greater urgency now. No matter what they had found in the testing, he had no time left to hunt. The next step on this one-way road was assignment and the signing of a release—the point of no return.

And through it all, something ate at his mind: some curious question, some phantom he could not pin down, a shadow figure which loomed up again and again in his mind, haunting him—the shadow of fearful doubt. Why the shock? Why had he broken loose? What had driven him to punish his arms and legs so mercilessly on the restrainers? What monstrous demon had torn loose in his mind? What gaping sore had the doctors scraped over to drive him to such extremes of fear and horror? *And why was the same feeling there in his mind whenever he thought of Paul Conroe?*

He sighed. He needed help and he knew it. He needed help desperately. Here, in a whirlpool of hatred and selfishness, he needed help more than he had ever needed it, help to track down this phantom shadow, help to corner it, to kill it. And the only ones he could ask for help were those around him, the Mercy Men themselves. He needed their help, if only to escape becoming one of them.

*

He dozed, then woke a little later and listened. There was an air of tension in the room, a whisper of something gone sharply wrong. Jeff forced himself up on his elbow, tried to peer through the darkness. Something had happened just before he awoke. He listened to the deathly stillness in the room.

And then he knew what it was. The breathing in the next room had stopped.

He lay back, his heart pounding, listening to the rasping of his own breath, fear and despair rising up to new heights in his mind. Death had come, then. One man who would never see the payoff he so eagerly awaited. Jeff had felt death pass over the room, and he knew, instinctively, that the entire unit would know it too without a single word passing from a single mouth. For the sense of death was a tangible thing here, moving with silent, imponderable footfalls from room to room.

For the first time, Jeff felt a kinship, a depth of understanding to share with the Mercy Men. And there was a depth of fear, deep down, which he knew now that he must share with them too. Painfully, he rolled over on his side and stared into the darkness for long minutes before he fell into fitful sleep.

CHAPTER NINE

A voice was talking across the room, a muffled, mysterious rumble of up-and-down sounds. Slowly Jeff dragged his mind out of the clinging depths of nightmare, back to the stuffy, dimly lit room. How long had he slept? And how late was it now? The soft voices across the room gave no clue, and his aching mind was too tired to care any more. He just lay in the dim light, every muscle aching, his mind returning again and again to the nightmare he had been reliving for the thousandth time.

It had been horribly sharp this time, clear as noonday: the same subject as always, the same face, the same horrible knowledge, and the same soul-wrenching hatred welling up and bubbling over in his mind. Always it was hatred without plan or form, pure, disorganized animal fury. But this time the dream had been more coherent, clearer, more unmistakable and vicious.

He had been walking down the street in the heart of the city. Yes, it was mid-morning. The sun's heat was unbearable already, and his jacket and shirt were damp. What was he doing that morning? Was he on his way to the survey depot with some information on the next Mars run? It didn't really matter. But he turned into the building and then it hit him.

It was like the shock that had struck him in the testing room, he thought. He had run into the man bodily. Stepping back to beg his pardon, he saw the man's face. That's where the dream went wild, just as his mind had gone wild on that sunny morning so long ago. He saw the man turn and run like the wind, snaking into the flowing stream of people on the street. Jeff followed, shouting, his fists and legs churning through the masses of people. He screamed in hoarse, maddened despair as he saw the figure vanish before his eyes.

And then he was leaning against the wall, panting, tears streaming down his face. Unable to understand, knowing only that this was the man whose face had haunted his dreams all his life, he acknowledged this was the man he would have to kill.

His eyes snapped open. The voices across the room were louder. Jeff listened. One voice was a woman's—Blackie's, of course. There was no mistaking the Nasty Frenchman's nasal twang. But the third voice—Jeff blinked his eyes. He moved his head to see the little group across the room.

They were huddled around a small infra-red coffee maker: Blackie, the Nasty Frenchman, and the huge, bald-headed man called Harpo. Blackie's voice was sharp and pleading as she echoed the Nasty Frenchman in angry protest. Harpo's heavy bass rumbled an undertone to the whispered discussion. Painfully, Jeff drew himself up on an elbow and turned his ear in the direction of the huddle, as the words drifted to him, unclearly:

"I say find out who and do something about it," the Nasty Frenchman was insisting angrily. His face was red and spiteful, and his eyes flashed as he glared up at Harpo. "We're out of it completely. Don't you see that? Because of this switch, we're off the payroll—ditched like common scum! Well, the job I've been on was to pay two hundred thousand dollars, with practically no risk involved. And I'll kill the man that's cutting me out of it."

Harpo's voice was soothing. "So maybe you're daydreaming. Maybe there won't be any switch of jobs at all."

"I saw the report, I tell you. It was signed by Schiml himself."

Harpo looked up sharply. "You actually saw Schiml's signature on it?"

"I saw it. I'm taken off assignment and so are you. We're both shoved out. Can't you get that straight? After all this time—and just because they get somebody in here that gets them excited."

Harpo snorted. "So they've gone off on these spook hunts before. Where do you think it'll take them this time? Extra-sensory powers!" The huge man spat in disdain. "Have you ever seen anybody with extra-sensory powers? Well, neither have I. Look, Jacques, let's face it: Schiml would give his left arm at the shoulder to have proof of extra-sensory powers in any form." Harpo grinned unpleasantly. "You've seen proof of that before. He believes in it, he wants to prove it. And every now and then he's going to have a try at it just to keep himself happy, just to keep in form. There's no call to get excited."

"But he's got a solid prospect this time," Blackie snapped. "From the stories I've heard the guy is a phenomenon. Hit top scores on the cards—highest they've ever recorded here. Other things too, like peeling the paper off the walls just by looking at them, or closing up opened wounds in ten minutes."

A MAN OBSESSED

"So you hear stories! Around here I don't believe anything I hear." Harpo shifted uneasily. "If there was anything tangible, anything we could put our hands on, I'd listen. But there's not—no proof, no nothing but a lot of wild stories. And I've even heard better stories in my time. You can't go around fighting stories—"

Jeff sat bolt upright, something shouting out in his brain. He grabbed for his shoes, oblivious to the agonizing pain in his muscles, fumbled eagerly, his mind screaming in excitement. "What kind of proof do you want?" he growled.

Harpo stared up at him, as though seeing a ghost. "You awake!" he gasped. And then: "Any kind of proof!"

"Then take a look at this." And Jeff tossed the crumpled card down in the middle of the huddle.

Blackie was on her feet, her eyes eager. "Didn't know you were anywhere near ready to wake up," she said. "You look like they really gave you the works."

"Well, something happened, all right. I don't know whether I'm coming or going."

Blackie nodded. "You never do, after testing. They came here for you, and I told them you'd gone out for a stroll. But I guess they found you." She put a cup of coffee in Jeff's hand and motioned toward the card. "You got that out of the file without being spotted?"

Jeff's eyes met hers for the briefest instant. "That's right. And I heard what you were talking about." He caught the little note of warning in her eyes: the silent, helpless appeal. He shook his head imperceptibly. He knew then that she hadn't told the others about their battle over the dice. He pointed to the card. "I think that answers a lot of things."

Harpo's eyes were suspicious. "How do you know that's the man?"

"Because I drove him in here, that's why." Jeff's voice was a snarl; it sounded sharp in the quiet room. "I knew he was here because he came here to escape me. But I didn't know he had any connection with ESP until I saw the card."

Harpo stared at the card, then at Jeff. "You mean you drove him in here?"

"That's right. Because I'd have killed him if he didn't come." Jeff's face was dark as he turned to the girl. "Tell him, Blackie. Tell him why I'm here."

Blackie told them. They listened with widening eyes, and the room was still as a tomb.

"And you came in here to kill this man—nothing more?" Harpo's voice was incredulous. "But man, you're on thin ice, very thin ice. If they tested you last night, you'll be assigned. Why, you could be forced to sign a release any time."

"I know it, I know it. Can't you see why there isn't time to bicker now?" Jeff's voice cracked in the still room, sharp and urgent. "This is the man, the one I'm looking for and the one you're looking for, the one with ESP that's got Schiml and his men so excited! It's here on the card!"

Harpo's eyes were narrow. "Any other proof besides the card that Conroe is the man?"

Jeff's voice was low with hate. "Look. I've been hunting the man down for five years. A long time. I've hunted him wherever he's gone. I've had the best detective agency in North America working with me hand and foot, tracking him down. But they haven't caught him. We've almost caught him, we've haunted him, we've run him back and forth across the country and world until he's ragged. But we've never caught him. Isn't there some significance to that? Time and again we've come so close that we couldn't miss—and then we missed. We've come too close too many times for coincidence. There's another factor, a factor that's giving Conroe warning, time after time. It's allowed him to slip out of perfectly sealed traps—*a factor like precognition, for instance.*"

There was a long silence. Then the Nasty Frenchman was on his feet, his lips stretched in a malicious grin. "If we move fast enough, we can stop it—cut it off at the bud. We're off the payroll now. But we can get back on it again, if their boy wonder dies."

Harpo's eyes flashed. "And how do you plan to do it?"

"Nothing simpler in the world. We just find the guy." The Nasty Frenchman's grin widened. "Then after we find him, we tell our friend Jeff about it. Nothing more. Jeff'll take it from there. Right, Jeff?"

Jeff's heart pounded against his ribs. "That's right," he said, his voice hoarse with eagerness. "Just find him for me."

Harpo bent over slowly, poured another cup of coffee. "Then let's talk plans," he said softly.

*

The planning went smoothly. Jeff sat forward eagerly. The despair and hopelessness of an hour before evaporated, leaving fingers of wild excitement creeping through his muscles, up and down his spine. These people knew where they were; they knew how to hunt in this evil place, where to go, what to do. This was the help he needed to complete his mission, the help he'd needed from the start. And now, at last, nothing would go wrong. Carefully, the last trap was laid—the final drive in this manhunt that had lasted so long and been so fruitless. This time there would be no slip.

Harpo fingered the card thoughtfully. "These dates must have some significance. Were there any signs of Conroe's visits here at those times?"

Jeff shook his head. "No sign. He couldn't have been here for more than three days at a time, or I'd have known about it."

Harpo grunted, his eyes sharp on Jeff's face. "And you had no definite, direct evidence that he was somehow using an extra-sensory talent in eluding you?"

Jeff scowled. "No direct evidence. I'm afraid not. There was no reason to suspect it, until I found the card. Then hindsight started filling in funny things that had gone unnoticed before."

Harpo nodded. "Yes. That's the way it would be. But Schiml must have had direct enough evidence. This ESP study is just like space travel was. They've been after it for years; they start after it time after time, every time a new angle comes up. Because if they succeed it could mean so much to so many people."

The Nasty Frenchman snorted. "Sure. Like running us out of paying jobs for good and all, after all the risks we've taken. Open the door to ESP for them, and there wouldn't be any other work in the Center for twenty years. And if we don't happen to be what they're looking for—" He ran his finger across his throat and scowled. "The man is here. We've got to have information on him, past and present. That means we'll have to search the Archives. There's no better approach." He turned his sharp little eyes on Jeff. "You know how the electronic files work. You're the one that can dig out what we need to know in the Archives."

Jeff nodded. "But I'll need time to work without interruption. Can you get me into the Archive files without being caught?"

The Nasty Frenchman nodded eagerly. "Nothing to it. Give us half an hour to clear the way and get the guards taken care of." He glanced up at Harpo. "The old fire-alarm gag should do it, all right. Then you can walk right down."

"And can you keep it clear for me, say, for an hour or so?"

"For five hours, if necessary." Harpo stood up sharply. "We'll start now to get things lined up. When it's clear, I'll give you a flicker on the phone. Don't answer it. Just come along. Blackie can draw you a map while you wait." The bald-headed giant started to leave, then turned back. "And don't let any alarm bells disturb you. We've found ways of occupying guards before." He touched his forehead briefly, and he and the Nasty Frenchman disappeared into the corridor.

*

"I think it'll work," Jeff breathed, tucking Blackie's crude penciled map into his pocket. "I think we've got him. Once we know where he is and what they're going to do with him—" He grinned up at her, his eyes shining. "His time's running out, Blackie. He's as good as dead."

The girl leaned forward, pouring coffee, sitting silently. Jeff watched her face, as if seeing it for the first time. Indeed, for the first time, the girl's face seemed softer. In the dim light of the room, the hard lines melted away, magically. Her face appeared younger and fresher, as though some curious mask had dropped away in the course of the evening.

But her eyes were troubled as she watched Jeff and lifted her coffee cup in mock salute. "To the Hunter," she said softly.

Jeff raised his own cup. "Yes. But not for long now."

"It can't go on much longer, Jeff. Your number's up next."

"For assignment?" Jeff's eyes flashed. "Do you think that makes any difference to me? I'm following through to the end on this, no matter what happens."

"But, Jeff, you can't sign a release."

Jeff stared at her in the silent room. "Why not? If it's the only thing I can do—"

Her eyes were wide and very dark. "Oh, Jeff, you're in terrible danger here."

79

A MAN OBSESSED

"I know that."

"You don't, you don't." The girl was shaking her head, tears rising to her eyes. "You don't know anything, Jeff, about the Mercy Men or the kind of work they do. Oh, I know, you think you do. But you don't, really. Look, Jeff—look at it straight—you're young, you're smart. There are other ways to spend your life, more important things for you to do. Can't you see that? No man is worth throwing your life away for, no matter what he's done to you. That's what you're doing. You're walking down a blind alley, into a death trap! Get out, while you can."

Jeff's head was shaking, his lips tight, until the color fled them, leaving pale gray lines. "I can't get out. I just can't. Nothing anyone could say could drive me out now."

"But you've got to run while you can! Oh, yes, go down there tonight if you must, try to find him. But if you don't find him, cut and run. Jeff, get out, tonight. They can't stop you; they have no legal hold on you, yet. But once they bring in a release, you're hooked. It'll be too late then."

Jeff's eyes narrowed, and he sat down on the bed and faced the girl. There was an elfin expression on her face, a curious intensity in her large gray eyes that he had never seen before. "What do you care?" he asked suddenly. "What do you care what I do?"

The girl's voice was low, and the words tumbled out so rapidly that he could hardly follow them. "Look, Jeff, you and me—we could work as a team. Don't you see what we could do? We could get out of here, together. We could get out of the city, go to the West Coast. The dice, think of the dice, man—we could clean up! You don't belong in here on the rack for slaughter. And I wouldn't belong here, either, if we could work together—"

Somewhere in the distance an alarm bell began ringing, insistently, clang-clanging down the corridors. Then there was a rush of feet, shouted orders and calls up and down the hallway, and the squeak of three jitneys passing by in rapid succession. Then, abruptly, the corridor fell silent again.

Jeff hardly noticed the clamor. He stared at the girl, his hands trembling. "Blackie, Blackie, think what you're saying. The tough-luck jinx. Have you forgotten? You're safe from it here. But outside, what would happen? We might make a go of it, yes, but what if the jinx followed us?"

"Oh, but Jeff, that's silly." She swallowed, her eyes almost overflowing as she tried to blink back the tears. "It isn't just selfishness, Jeff. I could stay here. I talked to Schiml this afternoon, before Harpo and Jacques started talking. They're out—yes. But I'm not. He wants me to stay, says there's a place for me in the work. But I don't want to stay."

Jeff was shaking his head slowly, his eyes tired. "It's no dice, Blackie. Not now. After I get Conroe, after I get out of here, then maybe I could think about it. But I haven't given this dice business any thought at all. Can't you see? I'd have to think it out, carefully, all its ramifications. And I haven't been able to do that. It hasn't mattered enough. I've got a man to kill, first, before anything else. And I'm going to kill him. I'm going to kill him tonight."

"Then do it for sure. Get him tonight! And then get out, before something happens—"

In the corner the phone gave two sharp rings, then lapsed into silence. Their eyes met, sharply, desperately. "Nothing's going to happen," Jeff said softly. "Don't worry about it. I've been at this too long for anything to happen."

There was a frantic light in the girl's gray eyes as she looked up at him, a depth and sincerity he had never seen before. Her eyes pleaded with him. "You don't know, you don't know...."

And then they were in each other's arms, drawing each other close, desperately. His hard lips met her soft ones, met and held. Then when they parted there was another look in her eyes, and he heard her breath cut sharply by his ear. "Jeff—"

Gently he put a finger to his lips, loosened her arms from around him. "Don't say it," he whispered. "Not now, Blackie. Not now—"

And then he was outside, in the corridor. The cool air caught him and he ran down the corridor toward the stairs. He hurried against the time the men had prepared for his safety. And as he ran, he felt his heart pounding in his ears, and he knew the hour was drawing close.

CHAPTER TEN

Jacques and Harpo were waiting for him at the head of the escalator. He nodded and followed them down the corridor to the small jitney car that was waiting.

"All set?"

"All set. The guards are all busy up in N unit putting out a fire. They won't be down to bother us for a couple of hours." The Nasty Frenchman scowled disdainfully. "But you'll have to hurry. When they come back, we'll have a time stalling them again."

Jeff nodded. "That should be enough. Then maybe we'll have other things to occupy the guards tonight."

The jitney started with a lurch and a squawk. Harpo handled the controls, running the little car swiftly down the corridor. It swung suddenly into a pitch-black tunnel, took an abrupt dip and began to spiral downward at a wild rate. Jeff grabbed the hand rail and gasped.

"It's a long way down," Harpo chuckled, sitting back in the darkness. "The Archives hold the permanent records of the entire Hoffman Center since it was first opened. That's why it's a vault, so that bombing won't destroy it. It's one of the most valuable tombs in history."

The jitney shot out into a lighted corridor. Jeff swallowed and felt his ears pop. The little car whizzed through a maze of tunnels and corridors. Finally it settled down to the floor before the heavy steel doors at the end of a large corridor.

Without a word, Harpo moved down to the end of the corridor, and drew the jitney car with him. He opened the motor hood, started pawing around busily inside.

The Nasty Frenchman chuckled. "If anyone wanders by, that jitney alarm siren goes off, and Harpo's just a poor technician trying to make it stop." The little man walked quickly to the steel doors. "It's not the first time I've had to work on these," he said slyly. "We wanted in here a few months ago, when they were trying to pull a shakedown deal on some of us. I worked out the combination pattern then; it took me three days. They change the combination periodically, of course, but the pattern is built into the lock."

He opened a small leather case and placed an instrument up against the lock. A long, thin wire was poised and ready in his other hand. Jeff heard several muffled clicks; then Jacques inserted the wire sharply into something. An alarm bell above the door gave one dull, half-hearted clunk and relapsed into silence, as though changing its mind at the last moment. A moment later the little Frenchman looked up and winked, and the steel vault door rolled slowly back.

The place smelled damp and empty. Three walls and half of the fourth were occupied with electronic file controls. The bulk of the room was taken up with tables, microviewers, readers, recorders, and other study-apparatus. There was nothing small in the room; the whole place breathed of bigness, of complexity, of many years of work and wisdom, of many lives and many, many deaths. It was a record-room that many lives had built.

Jeff moved in toward the control panel. He located the master coder and sat down in a chair before it, his eyes running over it carefully, sizing up the mammoth filing machine. And then, quite suddenly, he felt terribly afraid. A knot grew in his stomach and a cold sweat broke out on his forehead. A face was again looming up sharply in his mind. It was the huge, ghoulish face that had come to him again and again in his dreams; the face full of hatred and viciousness—pale and inhuman.

It was the face of a heartless, pointless, bloody assassin. But was that all? Or was there more to that face, more to that dream than Jeff had ever suspected? Something deep in his mind stirred, sending a chill down his spine. His hand trembled as he ran a hand over the control panel. A ghost was there at his elbow, a ghost that had followed him on this nebulous trail of bitterness and hatred for so long—a trail which would end in this very room.

He shook his head angrily. There was no time for panic, no time for ruminating. He picked the panel-code combination for the Mercy Men and the research unit. Then he computed the coding for Conroe's name. With trembling fingers, he typed out the coding, punched the tracer button and sat back, his heart thumping wildly. He watched the receiver slot for the telltale file cards and folio.

The file squeaked and chattered and whirred and moaned, and finally the pale instruction panel lighted up: No Information.

Jeff blinked, a chill running up his back. These files were the final appeal; the information had to be here. Quickly, he computed a description coding, fed it in and waited again in mounting tension. Still no information. He picked the code card from his pocket, the card from the Mercy Men's file up above, the card with the Hoffman Center's own picture of Conroe on it. He fed it into the photoelectric tracer, marked in the necessary coding for an unlimited file search: "Any person resembling this description in any way: any information on—" Again he sat back, breathing heavily.

The whirring went on and on. Then, inexorably, the little panel flickered and spelled out a single word:

"Unknown."

Jeff choked. He stared at the panel, his whole body shaking, and went through the coding again, step by step, searching for an error, finding none. It was impossible, it couldn't be so—and yet, the files were empty of information. As though there had never been a Paul Conroe. There was not even a reference card to the card in the Mercy Men's files.

He stared at the panel, his mind rebelling in protest. Nothing, not even a trace in the one place where there had to be complete information. He had come to a dead end—the last dead end there could be in the Hoffman Center.

The Nasty Frenchman lit a cigarette and watched Jeff from bright eyes. "No luck?"

"No luck," said Jeff, brokenly. "We're beaten. That's all."

"But there must be—"

"Well, there's not!" Jeff slammed his fist down on the table with a crash, his eyes blazing. "There's not a trace, not a whisper of the man in here. There has to be—and there's not. It's the same as every other time: a blank wall. Blank wall after blank wall. I'm getting tired of them, so miserably tired of running into blind alley after blind alley." He stood up, his shoulders sagging. "I'm too tired of it to keep it up. There's no point to gambling any longer. I'm getting out of here while I've got a whole skin."

"Maybe you've got more time than you think." The Nasty Frenchman eyed him in alarm. "This is no time to run out. It may be weeks before you're assigned."

Jeff stared at him. "Well, I know one way to find out." He walked over to the control panel, stabbed an angry finger at the master coder, picked out the coding for "J. Meyer." "They'll have me here too," he snapped. "The whole works about me: what the testing said, what they're going to do to me. That's one way to find out." Quickly, he typed out the coding, punched the tracer button....

The machinery whirred again, briefly. Then there was a click in the receiver slot and another and another. Jeff blinked at it as the microfilm rolls continued to fall down. Then he reached out to the single white card which fell on top of the rolls. His fingers were damp as he took the card. His own death warrant, perhaps? He glanced at the card and froze. His head began pounding as if it would burst.

"J. Meyer" he had punched in, and that was what the card said—*but not Jeffrey Meyer*. The card held a photo of a middle-aged, gray-haired man, and the typewritten name at the top said: JACOB MEYER.

And the picture was a photograph of his father's face.

*

It was impossible, incredible, but he stared at the card in his hand. It did not disappear; it stayed there. It still said: "Jacob Meyer"; it still showed the beloved features of his father, staring up at him blankly from the card. *His father!*

His heart pounded as he stared at the brief typewritten notation below the picture: "Born 11 August, 2050, Des Moines, Iowa; married 3 Dec. 2077, wife died childbirth 27 November 2078; one son Jeffrey born 27 November 2078." Then below were a series of dates: date of bachelor's degree, date of Master's and Doctorate; Associate Professor of Statistics at Rutgers University, 2079-2084; joined Government Bureau of Statistics in 2085. Finally, at the bottom of the card were a long series of reference numbers to microfilm files.

Jeff sank down in the chair, his mind spinning helplessly. He turned dazed eyes to the Nasty Frenchman. "You might as well go," he said. "I've got to do some reading."

Feverishly, he scooped up the microfilm rolls, carried them to the nearest reader, twisted the spool into the machine and bent his eyes to the viewing slot, his heart pounding in his throat....

A MAN OBSESSED

The first roll was a long, detailed series of abstracts of statistical papers, all written by Jacob A. Meyer, Ph.D., all covered with marginal notes in a scrawling, spidery hand and initialed "R.D.S." The papers covered a multitude of studies; some dealt with the very techniques of statistical analyses themselves, others were concerned with specific studies that had been done.

The papers were written in scholarly manner, perfectly well documented, but the marginal notes found fault continually, both with the samplings noted and the conclusions drawn. Jeff read through some of the papers and he scowled. They dated over a period of the four years when his father had been teaching statistics. There were several dozen papers, all with marginal notes, none of which made much sense to Jeff. With a sigh, he pulled out the roll, fed in another.

This one seemed a little more rewarding. It was a letter, signed by Roger D. Schiml, M.D., dated almost twenty years before, addressed to the Government Bureau of Statistics. Jeff's eyes skimmed the letter briefly, catching words here, phrases there:

... as director of research at the Hoffman Center, considered it my duty to bring this unbelievable condition to the attention of higher authorities.... Naturally, a statistical analysis must be made of the matter before it can be concluded that there has been a marked increase in mental illness of any kind in the general populace ... have followed Dr. Meyer's analyses in the past with much interest, and would be pleased if he could come to the Hoffman Center within the next month to commence such a study....

There was nothing tangible, nothing that made sense. Jeff shuffled through the rolls, popped another into place in the reader. This time he read much more closely a letter from an unknown person to Dr. Schiml. It was dated almost a year later than the former letter. This note referred in several places to the "Almost unbelievable results of the statistical study done several months ago." It also referred to the investigation just concluded of possible disturbing elements in the analysis. The final paragraph Jeff read through three times, his eyes nearly popping.

There was no doubt that the data was sound, and properly collected; naturally, the results of the analysis followed mathematically from the data. It seemed, therefore, that we were dealing with a disturbing factor heretofore quite unsuspected. Our investigation leads us to the inavoidable, though hardly credible, conclusion that Dr. Jacob A. Meyer *was himself* the sole disturbing factor in the analysis. No other possibility fits the facts of the picture. We recommend therefore that an intensive study of Dr. Meyer's previous work be undertaken, with a view to answering the obvious questions aroused by such a report. We also recommend that this be undertaken without delay.

At the top of the letter, in red letters, was the government's careful restriction: TOP SECRET.

Another roll went into the reader. This held the letter-head of a New York psychiatrist. Jeff's eyes caught the name and he read eagerly:

Dear Dr. Schiml:

We have studied the microfilm records you posted to us with extreme care, and undertaken the study of Jacob Meyer, as instructed. Although it is impossible to make a positive diagnosis without interviewing and examining the patient in person, we are inclined to support your views as stated in your letter. As to the possibility of other more remarkable phenomena occurring, we are not prepared to comment. But we must point out that this man almost certainly undergoes a regular manic-depressive cycle, may be dangerously depressed, even suicidal, in a depressive low, and may endanger himself and others in a manic period of elation. Such a person is extremely dangerous and should not be allowed freedom to go as he chooses.

Jeff looked up, tears streaming from his eyes. His whole body was wet with perspiration. He could hardly keep his balance as he stood up. What lies! The idea that his father could have been insane, that he could have falsified any sort of statistical report that he had done—it was impossible, a pack of incredible lies. But they were here, on the files of the greatest medical center on the face of the earth—lies about his father, lies that Jeff couldn't even attack because he could not understand them.

The door swung open sharply, and the Nasty Frenchman stuck his head in, panting. "Better get going," he snarled. "There are guards coming." His head disappeared abruptly, and Jeff heard Harpo's voice bellow at him: "Come on, we've got to run!"

Jeff's legs would hardly move. He felt numb as though a thousand nerve centers had been suddenly struck all at once. He fumbled, pouring the microfilm rolls into his pockets, his mind whirling. There was no sense to it: no understanding, no explanation. Somehow, he knew, there was a tie-in between these records of his father, taken so long ago, and the absence of any information on Paul Conroe in the files. But he couldn't find the link.

He ran out into the hall, leaped into the jitney car. He hung on for dear life as it sped up through the tunnel, into the blackness of the spiral once again. Suddenly, in his ears, another sound exploded, the loud, insistent clang of an alarm bell.

Harpo looked at the Nasty Frenchman and then at Jeff. "Oh, oh," he said softly. "They're onto something; that's a general muster. We'd better get back to quarters—and fast!"

He shoved the controls ahead a bit further, and Jeff felt the car leap ahead. Finally it settled down in the quarters corridor. They leaped out, Harpo set the dials for the car to return, and the three men ran for their quarters, the bell still clanging in their ears.

In Jeff's mind thoughts were tumbling as he ran—hopeless thoughts, uneasy thoughts. As he had ridden up, little chinks had fallen into place in his mind. Little spaces that he had never understood suddenly began to make sense, adding up to questions, big questions. It was too pat, too easy that Conroe should come in here and vanish as if he had never been alive. Things didn't happen that way, not even for Conroe.

Other things came into focus, slowly, flickering briefly through his mind—things that had happened years before, things that seemed, suddenly, to mean something. Then, just as they came into focus, they flickered back out of reach again. They were incidents like the night in the gambling room; like the night in the nightclub with the dancer swaying before him; like the sudden, shocking jolt that had awakened him from the depths of hypnosis and driven him face-first into a stone wall; things like the curious viciousness of his hatred for Paul Conroe—a hate that had carried him to the ends of the earth. But now that hate lay stalemated, and new and more frightening information threatened to descend on him.

What did it mean?

Jeff felt the uneasiness crystallize into real fear. He broke into a run down the corridor toward his room. Fear pounded through his mind, suddenly, unreasonably. He tore open the door, fell inside, closed it tight behind him before snapping on the lights.

The room was empty. The coffee pot still stood on the little table. It was still hot, still steaming. Blackie was gone and a cigarette still burned on the edge of the tray.

He had to get out! He knew it then, knew that was at the bottom of the unreasonable fear. The bell was still clanging in the hallway, loudly piercing the still air of the room. He had to flee while he could. Instinctively now he knew that he'd never find Paul Conroe in the Center, never in a thousand years of searching. The fear grew stronger, a little voice screaming in his ear, "*Don't wait. Run, run now, or it's too late.*"

He tore open his foot locker, stared at the empty hooks. The locker was cleaned out, empty of every stitch of clothing. His bag was gone, his shoes, his coat.

It's too late. Don't wait.

His pulse pounded in his temples and a sweat broke out on his forehead. The escalator! If he could get to it, then make the turn into the next corridor, and get a jitney car.... It was the only way to get out and he had no choice. Panting, he broke out into the hall once again, ran pell-mell down the corridor toward the escalator. Then, when he was almost there, a wire cage slammed down across the corridor and blocked his path completely.

Jeff stopped short, his shoes scraping against the concrete floor. His heart pounded a deafening tattoo in his ears as he stared at the wire grill. Then he whirled and ran back down the corridor as fast as his legs would move. If he could get back to the offices, back to the main corridor before they stopped him, he could get a car there. Far ahead he saw the bright light of the main corridor. His breath came in a hoarse whine as he tried to run faster. And then, ten yards ahead, he saw another grill clank down, cutting him off, falling directly in his path.

He cried out, a helpless, desperate cry. He was trapped, caught in the one length of corridor. His mind spun dizzily to Blackie. She had been gone. Where to? Where had everybody gone? He started back, frantically jerking open doors on either side of the corridor, staring into room after room, his breath catching in his throat as he ran. All the rooms were empty. Jeff felt his mind spinning. He felt a curious inevitability, a fantastic pattern falling into shape as he stared into the empty rooms. Finally he reached his own again. Wide-eyed and panting, he threw the door open, strode in and threw himself down in the chair and waited.

He did not wait long. For a few moments there was no sound. Then he heard the sounds of feet coming down the corridor. He tightened his grip on the chair arm. He wasn't thinking any longer. Cold beads of sweat stood out on his forehead as he waited, hearing the steps draw nearer. For the first time that he could remember, sheer terror crept through his mind, paralyzing him. He knew he had waited too long. His chance to jump the road was gone; there was no longer any escape.

Then the door was filled by some figures. One of them was the tall, white figure of Dr. Schiml. He walked into the room and smiled like the cat that ate the canary. Sinking down on the bed with a sigh, he was still smiling at Jeff. The girl followed him into the room. Her eyes were downcast. She tossed a little pair of ivory dice into the air and caught them as they fell.

The doctor smiled, and drew a crisp white paper from his pocket, began unfolding it slowly. "A matter of business," he said, almost apologetically. "It's time we got down to business, I think."

CHAPTER ELEVEN

Jeff raised his eyes to the doctor's face. His throat felt like sandpaper. He tried to swallow and couldn't. "Sorry," he grated. "I've changed my mind. I'm not talking business."

Dr. Schiml smiled, his head slowly moving back and forth. "I hear you're quite handy at the dice, Jeff."

Jeff jumped out of the chair, fists clenched, eyes blazing at the girl. "You bitch," he snarled. "You two-bit tramp stoolie. You'd sell your grandmother short for a bag of salt, wouldn't you? Come to me with your sob stories, beg me to move out of here with you." His voice was biting. "How much did they pay you to sell out? A hundred thousand, maybe? Or was this just a little routine affair? Maybe a thousand or two?"

The girl's face darkened, her eyes bewildered as she stared at him. "No, that's not true. I didn't—"

"Well, it won't do them any good, no matter how much they paid you. Because I'm not signing a release, now or ever."

A guard grabbed Jeff's arm, forcing him back into the chair.

Dr. Schiml still smiled, clasping his knee with his hands. "I guess you didn't quite understand me," he said pleasantly. "You mustn't blame Blackie. She didn't sell you short. She just couldn't help answering a few perfectly innocent questions." His eyes returned to Jeff, coldly. "We're not asking you to sign a release, Jeff. We're telling you."

Jeff stared at him in amazement. "Don't be silly," he blurted. "I'm not signing a release to you people. Do you think I'm out of my mind? Take it away, burn it and get yourself another guinea pig."

Dr. Schiml smiled quietly and shook his head. "We don't want another guinea pig, Jeff. That's just it. We want you."

A little line of sweat broke out on Jeff's forehead. "Look," he said hoarsely. "I'm not signing anything, do you understand? I've changed my mind. I don't care for the work here. I don't like the company."

Schiml's smile faded. He shrugged and tucked the white paper back into his white coat. "Just as you wish," he said. "The release is just a formality. Bring him along, boys."

"Wait!" Jeff was on his feet again, facing the guards, his eyes wide with fright. His eyes caught Schiml's. "Look, you've got things wrong. I'm a fake in here, a fraud. Can't you understand that? I didn't come in here to volunteer. I never intended to volunteer, never planned to go even as far as I did. I came here—"

Schiml made an impatient face and held up a hand. "Oh, yes, yes, I know all that. You came into this place because you'd followed a man in here and you wanted to kill him. You'd been hunting him for years, because you thought he murdered your father in cold blood and nothing would do but you kill him. Right?" Schiml blinked at Jeff, his voice heavy with boredom. "So you came in here and went through testing, hunting down your man, trying to find him. But you *didn't* find him. Now things have suddenly become too hot for your liking, so you figure that it's time to pull out. Right? Or are some of the details wrong?"

Jeff's jaw sagged, his face going pasty. "That slut girl—"

Schiml grimaced. "No, not Blackie. Blackie is discreet, in her own quiet way. She hasn't had anything to do with it. We've known about you all along, Jeff. And through a much more reliable source than Blackie." He glanced over his shoulder at one of the guards. "Bring him in," he said abruptly.

The door to the adjoining room opened and a man walked into the room. He was a tall, lean man; a gaunt-faced man with sallow cheeks and large, sad eyes; a weary-looking man whose hair was graying about the temples—a man whose whole body looked desperately tired.

And Schiml looked at the man and then he looked at the ceiling. "Hello, Paul," he said softly. "There's someone here who's been looking for you—"

A scream broke from Jeff's lips as he stared across the room. A raw animal scream ripped from his mouth like a knife. His lips twisted and he wrenched at the guards who were holding his arms, his face going purple, his eyes bulging.

With a roar he lunged at Conroe, bellowing, a torrent of hatred and abuse pouring from his lips. Again and again he screamed, his eyes blazing with an unholy fire of hatred. Conroe jerked back with a cry, and then Schiml was on his feet as Jeff lunged again, his muscles tightening like bands of steel under the flimsy shirt.

The guards fought to restrain him, and then the doctor was holding him too, crying: "Get out, Paul, quick!"

But Paul Conroe stood stock still, writhing from his hands to his head, his eyes filling with horrible pain. Suddenly the coffee cup jerked from the table, spun in the air and hurled straight for Conroe's head. It missed, smashing against the wall.

Jeff screamed again and the walls and ceiling began powdering off, plaster peeling down in great chunks, smashing off the walls onto the floor. A huge chunk fell from the ceiling, and then the curtains suddenly started to blaze, as if ignited by some magic fire. Finally, Conroe's clothing began smoking and smoldering.

Blackie screamed, staring at Jeff in open horror. Schiml's voice roared through the bedlam: "Get him! Sedate him, for God's sake, before he tears the place down on our ears!" Again Jeff roared his virulent hatred, and this time Conroe was the one who shouted:

"Stop him! He's tearing me apart inside. My God, stop him!"

Someone stepped between Jeff and Conroe. There was a flicker of glass and silver as a plunger was pressed home. Then suddenly Jeff's muscles gave out. His legs walked out from under him, and he felt himself sliding to the floor. But still he screamed, the face of the man who had tormented him all his life growing closer and closer, more and more vicious. Then suddenly everything around him went black. His last conscious impression was that of Blackie. She had her face in her hands and she was sobbing like a child in the corner.

*

He lay on the long table, wrapped in cool green surgical linens, motionless, barely breathing. His eyes were wide open, but sightless. They seemed to be staring straight up at the pale, glowing skylight in the ceiling. It was as if they were staring beyond, eons beyond, into some strange world that no human foot had ever trod.

His breath came slowly, a harsh sound in the still room. Sometimes it slowed almost to a stop, sometimes it accelerated. Dr. Schiml paused motionless by his side, waiting, watching breathlessly until the ragged wheeze slowed once again to normal.

Jeff lay like a corpse, but he was not dead. Near his head the panel of tiny lights flickered on and off, brighter and dimmer, carrying their simple on-or-off messages from the myriad microscopic endings on the tiny electrode that probed through the soft brain tissue.

A MAN OBSESSED

No human being could ever analyze the waxing and waning of patterns on that panel, not even in five lifetimes. But a camera could film the changes, instant upon instant, flickering and flashing and glowing dully on and off, in a thousand thousand different figures and movements. And the computer could take these patterns from the film and analyze them and compare them. It would integrate them into the constantly changing picture that appeared on the small screen by the bedside.

It was a crude instrument, indeed, for the study of so exquisitely delicate and variable an instrument as a human brain, and no one knew this more painfully than Roger Schiml. But even such a crude instrument could probe into that strange half-world that they had sought so long to enter.

Near the bedside Paul Conroe sat motionless, his face drawn, his gaunt cheeks sunken. His eyes were wide and fearful as he watched the picture panel and his fingers trembled as he lit his pipe. He kept watching.

"It could be so dangerous," he murmured finally, turning to look at Schiml. "So terribly dangerous."

Schiml nodded gravely, adjusting the microvernier that controlled the probing instrument. "Of course it could be dangerous, but not too much so. Twenty years ago he'd have been dead already, but we haven't been wasting time all these years we've been waiting for him. Particularly in this cell-probing technique, we've ironed out the bugs. He'll survive, all right, unless we run into something mighty—"

Conroe shook his head. "Oh, no, no. I don't mean dangerous for him. I mean dangerous for us. Even he doesn't realize his power. How can we predict what sort of power it might be?" He looked up at Schiml, his eyes wide. "That room—it would have been gone in another five minutes, simply torn apart into molecular dust. He did it—and yet, I'd swear he didn't know what he was doing. I doubt if he even realized what was happening. And the fire—that was real fire, Roger. I know, I felt it burn me."

Schiml nodded eagerly. "Of course it was real fire! Set molecules to spinning at terrifically accelerated rates and you have fire. But those are the things we have to learn, Paul."

Conroe shook his head, fearfully. "We could both see the fire, but there was something else. You couldn't feel the hatred that was in that room. I could." He looked up, his eyes haunted. "God, Roger, how could a man hate that way? It was thick; it ran out into the room like syrup. Oh, I've felt hatred before in the minds I've contacted, many times. I've felt vile hatred before, but this was alive, crawling hate—" He sighed, his hands trembling. "It's in his mind, Roger. We don't know what else he might do, even under anesthetic, if we hit the right places. But it's in his mind. That we know. But why?"

Schiml nodded again. "That's the key question, of course. Why does he hate you so much? When we know that"—the doctor spread his hands—"we'll have the answer to twenty years' work, perhaps. And dangerous as it is, we've got to find out, while we have a chance, Paul. You know that. We can't stop now, not with what we know. We know that Jeff's insanity is far less active right now than his father's was. But unless we can locate the areas, find the location of both factors, the psychosis and the extra-sensory powers, we're lost. We'd have no recourse but to turn our findings over to the authorities. And you know what that would mean."

Conroe nodded wearily. "Yes, I know. Mass slaughter, sterilization, fear, panic—all the wrong answers. And even the panic alone would be fatal in our psychotic world."

Dr. Schiml shrugged and went back to the bedside. "We'll know soon, one way or the other," he said softly. "We're coming through right now."

CHAPTER TWELVE

The needle moved, probed ever so slightly, stimulating deep, deep in the soft, fragile tissue ... seeking, probing, recording. A twinge, the barest trace of shock, a sharp series of firing nerve cells, a flicker of light, a picture—Jeff Meyer shifted, his eyelids lowering very slightly, and a muscle in his jaw began twitching involuntarily....

*

He was floating gently on his back, resting on huge, fluffy, billowing clouds. He didn't know where he was, nor did he care. He just lay still, spinning gently, like a man in free fall, feeling the gentle clouds around him pressing him downward and downward. His eyes were closed tightly—so tightly that no ray of light might leak in. He knew as he floated that whatever happened, he dare not open them.

But then there were sounds around him. He felt his muscles tighten and he clasped his chest with his arms. There were *things* floating through the air around him, and they were making little sounds: tiny squeaks and groans. He shuddered, suddenly horribly afraid. The noises grew louder and louder, whispering into his ear, laughing at him.

He opened his eyes with a jolt, staring at the long, black, hollow tunnel he was falling through. He was spinning, end over end, faster and faster down the tunnel. He strained to see through the darkness to the bottom, but he couldn't. Then the laughter started. First little, quiet giggles, quite near his ear, but growing louder and louder—unpleasant laughs, chuckles, guffaws. They followed each other, peal upon peal of insane laughter, reverberating from the curved tunnel walls, growing louder and louder, more and more derisive. They were laughing at him—whoever they were—and their laughs rose into screams in his ears. Then to gain silence he was forced to scream out himself. And he clasped his hands to his ears and shut his eyes tight—and abruptly the laughter stopped. *Everything* stopped.

He lay tense, listening. No, not everything. There were some sounds. Somewhere in the distance he could hear the bzz-bzz-bzz of a cicada. It sounded sharp in the summer night air. He rolled over, felt the crisp sheets under him, the soft pillow, the rustling of the light blanket. Where?...

And then it came to him, clearly. He was in his room, waiting, waiting and expecting.

Daddy! Quite suddenly, he knew that Daddy had come home. There had been no sound in the dark house; he hadn't even heard the jet-car go into the garage, nor the front door squeak. But he had known, just the same, that Daddy was here. He blinked at the darkness, and little chills of fright ran up his spine. It was so dark, and he didn't like the dark, and he wished Daddy would come up and turn on the light. But Daddy had said ever since Mommy died that he must be a brave little man, even if he was only four....

He lay and shivered. There were other noises: outside the window, in the room—frightening noises. It was all very well to be a brave little man, but Daddy just didn't understand about the dark and the noises. And Daddy didn't understand about how he wanted somebody to hold him close and cuddle him and whisper to him.

And then he heard Daddy's step on the stair and felt him coming nearer. He rolled over and giggled, pretending to be asleep. Not that he'd fool Daddy for a minute. Daddy would already know he was awake. They played the same game night after night. But it was fun to play little games like that with Daddy. He waited, listening until he heard the door open, and the footsteps reach his bed. He heard Daddy's breathing. And then he rolled over and threw the covers off and jumped up like a little white ghost, shouting, "Boo! Did I scare you, Daddy?"

And then Daddy took him up on his shoulders and laughed, and said he was a big white horse come to carry little Jeff on a long journey. So they took the long journey down to the study for milk and cookies, just as they always did when Daddy came home. He knew Daddy didn't want any milk, of course. Daddy never drank milk at night with him. Daddy was much more interested in the funny cards, the cards he had watched Daddy make that day a year ago. Daddy had him run through them over and over and over ... circle, spiral, figure eight, letter B, letter R.... *It was a letter R, Daddy? But it couldn't have been, I know—oh, you're trying to catch me! Can we play with the marbles now, Daddy? Or the dice tonight? The round-cornered ones—they're much easier, you know.*

But Daddy would watch him as he read the cards, wrinkling up his nose and calling out the figure. And he would see Daddy mark down each right one and each wrong one. And then he would feel Daddy almost beaming happiness and satisfaction. And he would wait eagerly for Daddy to get out the dice, because they were so much more fun than the cards. *The square-cornered dice, Daddy? Oh, Daddy, they're so much harder. Oh, another game, a new one? Oh, good, Daddy. Teach me a new game with them, please. I'll try very hard to make them come out right.*

And then after the new game, Daddy told him a story before bed. It was one of his funny stories, where he *talked* the story, but put in all the fun and jokes and private things without any words.

It was funny. None of the others, like Mary Ann down the block, could feel their daddies like he could. Sometimes he wondered about it. He would tell Mary Ann about it as a special secret, but she wouldn't believe him. Nobody can hear their daddies without their daddies talking, she said. But he knew better.

And then there were thoughts creeping through his mind, feelings coming from Daddy that were uncomfortable feelings. He sat up suddenly in Daddy's arms and felt the chill pass through him.

"Daddy...."

"Yes, son."

"Why—why are you afraid, Daddy? What are you afraid of?"

And Daddy laughed and looked at him in a strange way and said, "Afraid? What do you mean, afraid?" But the afraidness was still there. Even when he went to bed and Daddy left him again, he could still feel the afraidness....

And then, abruptly, he was swinging into a vast, roaring whirlpool that swung around his head. He felt his body twisting in the blackness, swirling about, carried along without effort. He knew, somehow, that he was Jeff Meyer. And he knew that the needle was there, probing in his mind; he could feel it approach and withdraw. He could feel the twinge of recognition, the almost intangible sudden awareness and realization of a truth.

Then the seeker was gone: the probe finished in that area and moved on to the next. The whirlpool was a tunnel of rushing water, swinging about him, whirling him with lightning speed up ... up ... up; around, then down with a sickening rush. Then up again, as though he were riding the Wall of Death in a circus, around and around ... yet always drawing him in closer ... closer ... closer....

To what?

He knew he was fighting it, twisting with all his strength to fight against the impossible whirlpool which choked and carried him like a feather. He clenched his fists and fought, gritting his teeth, desperate, suddenly horribly afraid, more horribly afraid than he had ever been in his life. Down at the end of the tumultuous whirlpool, something lay—something horrid and ugly, something that had been wiped out of his mind, scoured out and disposed of long, long ago. *It was something he dared not face, never again.* Suddenly Jeff screamed and tried to force his mind back to that place. He tried desperately to remember, tried to see where the whirlpool was leading him before it was too late—*before it killed him!*

Something lay down there, waiting for him. It was more hideous than his mind could imagine—*something which could kill him.* Closer and closer he swept, helpless, his body growing rigid with fear, fighting, blood rushing through his veins. But he couldn't escape that closed, frantic alleyway to death.

Daddy was afraid. The thought screamed through Jeff's mind with the impact of a lightning bolt. It paralyzed his thoughts, tightened his muscles into rigid knots. Daddy was afraid ... afraid ... *afraid*—so horribly afraid.

The thought swept through him, congealing his blood. He cried out, shaking his head, trying to fight away the seeping stench of deadly fear, trying to clear it out of his mind. His face twisted in agony and his whole body wrenched. Suddenly, he was screaming and pounding his face against the ground. He was alone and his mind was wracked and obsessed by that horrible fear.

He opened his eyes and saw the turf under his head. Dimly, through the pain sweeping through his mind, he saw the grassy meadow on which he lay, completely by himself. The little singing brook was a few feet away. The afternoon sun was high, but the willow tree hung over him, covering him with cool shade. From somewhere a bird was singing.

"Daddy!" The word broke from his lips in a small scream, and he sat bolt upright, his hair tousled, his small, keen-featured eight-year-old face twisted with the pain and fear that tore through his mind. Some corner of his brain, so very remote, told him that he was not eight, that he was a grown man. But he saw his tiny hands, grubby with the dirt of the barnyard and lane through which he had walked in coming here. He had been driven here by the pain and fear and hatred that had been streaming into his mind.

It was Daddy. He knew it was Daddy, and Daddy was afraid. Daddy was running, with the desperation of a hunted animal, running down a corridor, his mind in a frenzy of fear. He was peering back over his shoulder, his breath coming in great gasps as he reached the end of the hall, wrenched vainly at the door and then collapsed against it. And while he sobbed in great gasps, tears of fear and desperation ran down his cheeks.

Jeff saw the door; he felt Daddy's body heaving, heard the furious pulse pounding in his own head. He saw the cold, darkened corridor, and his mind was picked up in the frenzied sweep of his father's thoughts, carried in a rush he could neither understand nor oppose. Stronger than ever before, his thoughts were Daddy's thoughts. He saw through Daddy's eyes; he felt through Daddy's body. In the closest rapport they had ever known, though Jeff lay here on the grassy plot, his body writhed with the pain and fear that Daddy was suffering miles distant.

They're coming, his mind screamed. *Trapped, trapped—what can I do?* Daddy was racing back up the corridor now, his eye catching an elevator standing open. He ran inside, groped frantically for the switch. He had to get away, had to get down below, somehow get to the street! Oh, God, what a mistake to walk into this place—an office building, of all places, where they could so easily follow him in, cut him off, trap him!

Why had he come? Why? He'd known they were hunting for him, knew they'd been getting closer and closer. But how could he have sensed that this day would bring a panic, that the stock market would take its nosedive this one particular day, putting the finger on him without any question, spotting him, pointing out his exact location to his hunters, beyond shadow of doubt?

How could he have known? This was to have been the final test, the test to prove the force he had in his mind—the force which had been destroying and destroying and destroying. And it had emanated from his own mind in some unspeakable way, uncontrolled, unbelieved and misunderstood. It was the force which had brought the hunters to him.

But not now! Oh, please, please, not now—not when he was so close to the answer. Not when he was so close. Slowly, helpless anger seethed through his mind. They had no right to stop him now. In another day, another week, he could have the answer. In another few days he would have corralled this frightening power, controlled it. He knew he could find the answer. He stood on the very brink. But now the hunters had trapped him—

Why, Daddy? Why are they hunting you? Oh, Daddy, Daddy, please, I'm so scared! Please, Daddy, come home. Please don't be so much afraid, Daddy. I'm so frightened....

The elevator gave a lurch. He fell against the door as the car ground to a halt between floors. Frantically, he pounded the button, waited through long eternities as the car sat, silent, motionless. Then his fingers ran hastily along the cracks in the car door, seeking a hold, trying desperately to wrench open the locked door.

He felt them coming, somewhere above him, somewhere below him. Then something tore loose in his mind; some last dam of control broke, and he was screaming his defiance at them, screaming his hatred, his bitterness. They had him, they were going to kill him without trial, shoot him down like a mad dog. He felt them flinch and cower back at the stream of hatred roaring out of his mind, felt them move back. They were afraid of him, but they were determined to kill him.

A sound above! He flattened back against the elevator wall, wrenching at the metal grating with superhuman strength, trying to twist open the metal, to find some way into the shaft below. Someone was coming down from above, down onto the top of the elevator; someone whose mind was filled with fear, but who moved with determination. There was a scraping sound from above, a dull twang of cable striking against cable.

They could be cutting the car loose.

He leaped for the ceiling of the car, stabbing up with his fingers for the little escape doorway. Sheer hatred drove his legs as he jumped and jumped again, until the door flew up. His hand caught the rim, and he dragged his body up. He jerked his shoulders through the small opening, heaving and lunging through to the top of the car.

He looked up. He saw a face, a single face, hanging mistily above him. Dimly he made out the form of a man hanging on the cable twenty feet above. His legs were wrapped around the cables and one hand carried the small, dully gleaming weapon. His mind screamed hatred at the man, and he grabbed at the cables, wrenching them, shaking them like a huge tree.

A MAN OBSESSED

He saw the man slowly moving down, spinning back and forth helplessly as the cables vibrated. But he held on tenaciously, moving closer.

Daddy! Stop him! Daddy, don't let him kill you.

The face came into clearer view: a thin face, an evil one, twisted with fear and pain. The figure moved slowly down the cables, slowly turning, lifting the arm with the weapon, patiently trying to take aim. It was a gaunt face, with high cheekbones, slightly bulging eyes, high flat forehead, graying hair. *Remember that face, Jeff. Never forget that face, that face is the face of the man who is butchering your father.* Hatred streamed out at the face; he crouched back against the wall of the shaft, wrenching at the cables, trying vainly to shake the killer loose. He had to get him first; he had to stop him. *He's so close; he's turning; the gun is raising. I'll never get him—*

The face, hovering close, eyes wide—the face of a ghoul—and below the face was the dull, round hole of the gun muzzle, just inches away. A finger tightened. A horrible flash came, straight in the eyes—

Daddy!

The thoughts screamed through his mind: the bitter, naked hatred, the hatred of madness, streaming out in one last searing inferno. Then came a sickening lurch, a lurch of maddened fear and hate. And there was the snuffing out of a light, leaving darkness....

Daddy! No, Daddy. No, I can't feel you any more, Daddy. What have they done to you? Oh, please, Daddy, talk to me. Talk to me. No, no, no. Oh, Daddy, Daddy, Daddy....

Dr. Schiml looked up from the pale, prostrate form after a long time; his forehead was beaded with sweat. The color had drained almost completely from Jeff's face, and his skin had taken a waxy cast. His breathing was so shallow it was hardly audible in the still room, and the panel of flickering lights had become almost completely still.

"We can't go on yet," said Dr. Schiml, his voice hoarse. "We'll have to wait." He turned and walked across the room, trying to keep his eyes away from the prostrate form on the bed; yet everywhere he went, it seemed his eyes caught the idiotic stare in the man's blank eyes. "We'll have to wait," he repeated, and his voice was almost a sob.

CHAPTER THIRTEEN

Paul Conroe moved for the first time, running a hand through his thick gray hair as he glanced up at Schiml. "Some of that came through to me, even now," he said weakly. His face, also, was ashen and his eyes were haunted. "To think that he hated me that much, and to think *why* he hated me—" He shook his head and buried his face in his hands. "I never knew about the old man and the son. I just never knew. If I'd known, I'd never have done it."

The room was still for a long moment. Then Schiml blinked at Conroe, his hands trembling. "So this is the tremendous power, the mutant strain we've been trying to trace for so long."

"This is one of the tremendous powers," Conroe replied wearily. "Jeff probably has all the power that his father had, though it hasn't all matured yet. It's just latent, waiting for the time that the genes demand of his body for fulfillment. Nothing more. And other people have the same powers. Hundreds, thousands of other people. Somewhere, a hundred and fifty years ago, there was a change—a little change in one man or one woman."

He looked up at Schiml, the haunted look still in his large eyes. "Extra-sensory powers—no doubt of it, a true mutant strain, but tied in to a sleeper—a black gene that spells insanity. One became two and two spread to four—extra-sensory power and gene-linked insanity. Always together, growing, insidiously growing like a cancer. And it's eating out the roots of our civilization."

He stood up, walked across the room and stared down at the pallid-faced man in the bed. "This answers so many things, Roger," he said finally. "We knew old Jacob Meyer had a son, of course. We even suspected then that the son might share some of his powers. But this! We never dreamed it. The father and son were practically two people with one mind, in almost perfect mutual rapport. Only the son was so young he couldn't understand what was wrong. All he knew was that he 'felt' Daddy and could tell what Daddy was thinking. Actually, everything that went on in his father's mind—*everything*—was in his mind too. At least, in the peak of the old man's cycle of insanity—"

Schiml looked up sharply. "Then there's no doubt in your mind that the old man was insane?"

A MAN OBSESSED

Conroe shook his head. "Oh, no. There was no doubt. He was insane, all right. A psychiatric analysis of his behavior was enough to convince me of that, even if following him and watching him wasn't. He had a regular cycle of elation and depression, so regular it could almost be clocked. He'd even spotted the symptoms of the psychosis himself, back in his college days. But of course he hadn't realized what it was. All he knew was that at certain times he seemed to be surrounded by these peculiar phenomena, which happened rapidly and regularly at those times when he was feeling elated, on top of the world. And at other times he seemed to carry with him an aura of depression. Actually, when he hit the blackest depths of his depressions, he would be bringing about whole waves of suicides and depression—errors and everything else."

Conroe took a deep breath. "We knew all this at the time, of course. What we didn't know was that the old man had been seeking the answer himself, actively seeking it. All we knew was that he was actively the most dangerous man alive on Earth, and that until he was killed he would become more and more dangerous—dangerous enough to shake the very roots of our civilization."

Schiml nodded slowly. "And you're sure that his destructive use of his power was a result directly of the insanity?"

Conroe frowned. "Not quite," he said after a moment. "Actually, you couldn't say that Jacob Meyer 'used' his extra-sensory powers. They weren't, for the most part, the kind of powers he could either control or 'use.' They were the sort of powers that just happened. He had a power, and when he was running high—in a period of elation, when everything was on top of the world—the power functioned. He fairly exuded this power that he carried, and the higher he rose in his elation, the more viciously dangerous the power became."

Conroe stopped, staring at the bed for a long moment. "The hellish thing was that it couldn't possibly be connected up with a human power at all. After all, how can one human being have an overwhelming effect on the progress of a business cycle? He can't, of course, unless he's a dictator, or a tremendously powerful person in some other field. And Jacob Meyer was neither. He was a simple, half-starved statistician with a bunch of ideas that he couldn't even understand himself, much less sell to anyone who could do anything with them. Or how can a man, *just by being in the*

104

vicinity, tip the balance that topples the stock market into an almost irreparable sag?"

Conroe leaned forward, groping for words. "Jacob Meyer's psychokinesis was not the sort of telekinesis that we saw Jeff turning against me in that room a couple of hours ago. He could probably have managed that, too, if he had hated me enough. But if Jacob Meyer's mind had merely affected physical things—the turn of a card, the fall of the dice, the movement of molecules from one place to another—he would have been a simple problem. We could have isolated him, studied him. But it wasn't that simple."

Paul Conroe sat back, regarding Schiml with large, sad eyes. "It would have been impossible to prove in a court of law. We knew it and the government knew it. That was why they appointed us assassins to deal with him. *Because Jacob Meyer's mind affected probabilities.* By his very presence, in a period of elation, he upset the normal probabilities of occurrences going on around him. We watched him, Roger. It was incredible. We watched him in the stock market, and we saw the panic start almost the moment he walked in. We saw the buyers suddenly and inexplicably change their minds and start selling instead of buying. We saw what happened in the Bank of the Metropolis that first day we tried for him. He was scared, his mind was driven into a peak of fear and anger; it started a bank run that morning that nearly bankrupted the most powerful financial house on the East Coast! We saw this one little man's personal, individual influence on international diplomacy, on finances, on gambling in Reno, on the thinking and acting of the man on the street. It was incredible, Roger."

"But surely Jacob Meyer wasn't the only one—"

"Oh, there were others, certainly. We've a better idea of that, now, after all these years of study. There were and are thousands and thousands—some like me, some much worse—all carrying some degree of extra-sensory power from that original mutant strain, all with the gene-linked psychosis paired up with it every time. And we've seen our civilization struggling against these thousands just to keep its feet. But Jacob Meyer was the first case of the whole, full-blown change in one man that we'd ever found. He was running wild, his mind was completely insane. And the extra-sensory powers he carried were so firmly enmeshed in the insanity that there was no separating the two. Meyer tipped us off. He set us on the trail, and the trail led to his son after he was dead—"

"Yes, the son. We have the son." Schiml scowled at the shallow-breathing form on the bed. "We should have had him before—years before."

"Of course we should. But the son vanished after his father's death. We never knew why he vanished—until now. But now we know that when we killed his father, we did more than just that. We almost killed our last chance to catch this thing and study it before it was too late. Because when we killed Jeff's father, *we killed Jeff Meyer too.*"

Schiml scowled. "I don't follow. He's still alive."

"Oh, of course he's still alive. But can't you see what happened to him? He was living in his father's mind; he knew everything his father knew—but he didn't understand it. He thought with his father's thoughts, he saw through his father's eyes, because they were mutually and completely telepathic. He felt his father's fear and frustration and bitterness when we trapped him in that office building finally. He lay screaming on the ground on a farm somewhere, but actually he was in his father's mind.

"It was a mad mind, a mind rising to the highest screaming heights of mania, as he waited for me to come down and kill him. And Jeff was surrounded with his father's hatred. He saw my face through his father's eyes, and all he could understand was that his daddy was being butchered and that I was butchering him. When the bullet went into his father's brain and split his skull open, Jeff Meyer felt that too. When his father died, Jeff died too—a part of him, that is. They were one mind and part of that one mind was destroyed."

Conroe paused, his forehead covered with perspiration. The room was silent except for the hoarse breathing of the man on the table. Conroe's face, as he looked down, was that of a ghost.

"No wonder the boy disappeared," he whispered. "He'd been shot through the head. He was almost virtually dead. He must have gone into shock for years after such a trauma, Roger. He must have spent years roaming that farm, cared for by an aunt or uncle or cousin, while he slowly recovered. No wonder we could find no trace. And then, when he did get well, all he knew was that his father had been murdered. He didn't know how; he didn't know why, and he dared never remember the truth. Because, the truth was that *he* had been killed. All he dared recognize was my face—a recurrent, nightmarish hallucination, rising out of his dreams, plaguing him on the streets, tormenting him day and night."

"But you were hunting him."

"Oh, yes, we were hunting him. It was inevitable that sooner or later we would come up face to face. But when we did, I received such a horrible mental blow that I couldn't even look to see what he looked like. I could do nothing but scream and run. When he saw me that day in the night club, he took complete leave of his senses. He exploded into hatred and bitterness. And then he resolved to hunt me down and kill me for killing his father."

Conroe spread his hands apologetically. "It seemed good sense to use that hatred and singleness of purpose to draw him here. But it was torture. He followed me with his mind, without even knowing it. It was old Jacob Meyer's face that haunted me everywhere I went. I didn't know why, then, because I didn't know Jeff had been part of that mind. And Jeff didn't know that he carried and broadcast that horror wherever he went."

Conroe leaned back, his body limp in exhaustion. "We needed Jeff so desperately. Yes, we needed him in here, for testing, for this study. It's been a long, tedious job, studying him, observing him, photographing him, learning how much of his father's power he had. And we dared not bring him in here until we were sure it was safe. And now, with what he knows, he is more vitally dangerous than his father ever was. There are hundreds that carry the change, in larger or smaller part, all gene-linked with insanity. And Jeff Meyer is insane as any of the rest of them. But at least there's hope, because we can study him now. Because unless we can somehow separate the function of the insanity from the function of the psychokinesis, we have no choice left, no hope."

Schiml looked up, his eyes wide. "No choice—"

"—but to kill them, every one. To hunt out the strain and wipe it from the face of the Earth so ruthlessly and completely that it can never rise again. And to wipe out with it the first new link in the evolution of Man since the dawn of history."

Slowly Roger Schiml's eyes traveled from Jeff Meyers' form on the bed to Paul Conroe's grave face. "There's no other way?"

"None," said Paul Conroe.

*

"Jeff," said Dr. Schiml. "Jeff Meyer."

The figure on the cot stirred ever so slightly. The eyes slowly closed, then reopened, looking slightly less blank. Jeff's lips parted in an almost inaudible groan, hardly more than a breath.

"Jeff. You've got to hear me a minute. Listen, Jeff, we're trying to help you. Can you hear that? We're trying to help you, Jeff, and we need your help."

The eyes shifted, turned to Schiml's face. They were haunted eyes—eyes that had seen the grave and beyond it.

"Please, Jeff. Listen. We're hunting. We're trying to find a way to help you. You know about your father now, the truth about your father, don't you?"

The eyes wavered, came back, and the head nodded ever so slightly. "I know," came the sighing reply.

"You've got to tell us what to do, Jeff. There are good powers here in your mind, and there are terrible powers, ruinous powers. We've got to find them both, find where they lie, how they work. You must tell us, as we probe—tell us when we strike the good, when we strike the bad. Do you understand, Jeff?"

Again the head nodded. Jeff's jaw tightened a trifle and an expression of infinite fatigue crossed his face. "Go on, Doc."

Dr. Schiml leaned over the proper controls and moved the dial on the microvernier. He moved it again, watching, moving it still again. A fine sweat broke out on his forehead as he worked, and he felt Conroe's soft eyes on him, waiting, hoping....

And then a whimper broke from Jeff's lips, an indefinable sound, helpless and childlike, a little cry of terror. Dr. Schiml looked up, his heart thumping in his throat. Jeff's eyes were wide again, staring lifelessly, and his breath was shallow and thready. Schiml glanced quickly at Conroe, then back, his eyes reflecting the fear and tension in his mind. And as he worked his shoulders slumped forward, prepared for defeat. Because what he was doing was impossible, and he knew it was impossible. But he knew, above all, that it had to succeed.

CHAPTER FOURTEEN

He was spinning like a top, end over end, as though he had sprung off a huge, powerful diving board. He rose higher and higher into the air. Lying tense, Jeff knew that his body was still on the soft bed, yet he felt his feet rising, his head sinking, as he spun head over heels through the blackness. And he could feel the tiny probing needle, seeking, hunting, stimulating....

A siren noise burst in his ears: a shimmering blast of screeching musical sound that sent cold shivers down his back. Then it leveled off to an up-and-down whine that gradually became a blat of static in his ear. Somewhere, out of the uneven grating of the noise, he heard a voice whispering in his ear, hoarsely. He paused, straining to hear, trying to catch an occasional word.

He knew that there were no voices outside of his body. He was sure of that. Yet he heard the sound, deeper in his ear, louder and softer, then louder again. It whispered to him, carrying a note of deepest urgency in the soft sibilants. Quite suddenly, it seemed vitally important to hear what the voice was saying, for the words were clearly directed at him. He shifted slightly and listened harder, until the words came through clearly.

And then he gasped, a feeling of panic sweeping through him. He heard the words and they were nonsense words, sounds without meanings. Something stirred in his mind, some vague memory of nonsense words, of a horrible shock. Had there been a shock? But the strange sounds frightened him, driving fear down through the marrow of his bones. The whispering sounds were sinister: babbling sounds, sounds of words that *needed* meaning and had none—half-words, garbled, twisted, meaningless.

Cautiously he opened his eyes, peered through the murky blackness to see the whisperers. His eyes fastened on two shapeless forms, tall, ghostly, in black robes with hoods drawn up over their faces. The figures leaned on their sticks and held their heads together. They babbled nonsense to each other with such fierce earnestness that they seemed somehow horridly ridiculous. Taking a deep breath, Jeff started toward the two figures, then stopped short, his heart pounding wildly in his throat.

Because the moment he had made a move toward them, the figures turned sharply toward him, and their nonsense voices had suddenly become clear for the briefest moment. They became clear and unmistakable and heavy with horrible meaning: "Stay away, Jeff Meyer. Stay away."

He stared about, trembling, trying to place himself, trying to find some landmark. The hooded figures turned back to each other and began babbling once again. But now they seemed to be standing before an archway—a gloomy, gray archway which they seemed to be guarding. Slowly, slyly, Jeff started to move away from them. But he watched them from stealthy eyes, and as he moved away the gloom about him cleared, and things were suddenly brighter. And then there was singing in his ears, joyous choruses bursting forth in happy song. A great feeling of relief and complacency settled down upon him like a mantle. He smiled and breathed deeper and started to roll over.

"*What was that, Jeff? What did we strike?*"

He shook his head violently, a frown creasing his face. "Stay away," he muttered. "The old men, they were there." Suddenly he felt himself twist around until he was facing the hooded figures again, and his feet were moving him toward them again, involuntarily, inexorably. And then the nonsense words settled out again, more menacingly, louder this time than before: "No closer, Jeff Meyer. Stay away—away—away."

"Can't go there," he muttered aloud.

"*Why not, Jeff?*"

"They won't let me. I've got to stay away."

"*What are they guarding, Jeff?*"

"I don't know. I don't know, I tell you. I've got to stay away!"

And then suddenly the singing dissolved into a hideous cacophony of clashing sounds, a din that nearly deafened him. A huge wave suddenly swept up around him. It was like a breaker at the ocean's edge, swirling up, surrounding him, catching him up and hurling him head over heels down a long, whirling tunnel. Desperately he fought for balance and finally found his feet under him once again. But then the ground was moving under him. He ran frantically, until his breath came in short gasps and his blood pounded in his ears. Then he caught a branch that swept by near him, and raised himself up as the flooding water roared underneath him.

The sky around him was clouding over blackly. Far in the distance he saw a blinding flash of lightning, ripping through the sky, bringing the bleak, wind-torn landscape into sharp relief in his mind as he clung to the branch. He heard a flapping of wings as a huge, black vulture skimmed by. And then the rain began to fall, a cold, soaking rain that ate through his clothes and soaked his skin. It ran in torrents into his eyes and ears and mouth.

And then he heard voices all around him. How could there be voices here? For there were no people, no sign of warm-blooded life. But there were voices, pleasant ones. They came from all sides. He could see no one, but he could *feel* them.

Feel them! He gasped in pure joy, shooting out his mind eagerly, unbelievingly, searching out the sudden feeling of perfect, warm *contact* he had just felt. And then his mind was running from person to person, dozens of persons, and he could feel them all, as clearly, as wondrously as he had ever felt his father—sharply, beautifully.

He cried out, he cried out for joy. Tears of unrelieved happiness rolled down his cheeks as he stretched out his mind and embraced the thoughts of the people he could feel but not see. And he felt his own thoughts being met, being caught and embraced and understood.

"Right here!" he shouted. "Schiml, this is it, don't lose it, man. This is the center. I'm controlling it. You've got it now. *Work it, Schiml. Work it for all you've got.* "

And then he looked at the black, menacing sky around him, and his mind laughed and cried out for the clouds to go away. And there was a wild whirling of clouds and they broke, and the sun was streaming down upon him suddenly. He threw himself from the tree, ran down the hillside. He felt a wonderful, overpowering freedom he had never felt before, his mind free to soar and soar without hindrance. There was nothing now to stand between it and complete understanding of all men. It was a mind which could go wherever he wanted it to go, do whatever he wished.

He ran down toward the bottom of the hill and felt his control growing with every step he took. He knew when he reached the bottom of the hill that the battle would be won, so he ran all the faster.

And then, like some horrible nightmare, the hooded figures loomed up directly in his path, long bony fingers stabbing out at him accusingly. He fell flat on his face at the overpowering warning in the voices that struck him. And he lay at the feet of the figures and sobbed, his whole body shaking with bitter, hopeless sobs. And the dark clouds gathered again. He was too late, too late.

"What are they guarding, Jeff?"

"I don't know. I don't know. I can't break through."

"You've got to, Jeff. You've got to! We've got the extra-sensory center. We've found it, but something is blocking it. Jeff, something is keeping you away. You've got to see what—"

"I can't. Oh, I can't. Please, don't make me!"

"You must, Jeff!"

"No!"

"Go on, Jeff."

He stood up, facing the hood figures, cowering, his whole body trembling. Deep in his mind he could feel the probing needle, moving, slowly moving, forcing him nearer and nearer to the grim figures. Slowly his feet moved, dragging in fear, a paralyzing fear that demanded every ounce of strength he possessed to make his legs function. And the voices, laden with menace, were grating in his ear, "Stay out, stay away. If you want to live, stay away ... away ... away...."

He moved closer and closer to the hooded figures, leaned forward to peer around them toward the gray, ghastly gate they guarded—a gate heavy with mold and rusty iron braces.

And then he reached up and threw back the hood of the first figure, stared at the face it had covered, and burst into a scream.

It was his own face!

He turned and threw back the other hood and peered intently, fighting to see the face before the features blurred out beyond recognition. It was his face, too, unmistakable. With a roar of anger and frustration he reached out, tore away the hoods, ripped them off, one with each hand, and wrenched away the enclosing shrouds.

The figures were skeletons with his face! He struck them and they shattered like thin glass, falling down in pieces at his feet. And he brushed his feet through the debris and turned to press his shoulder against the gate, heaving against it until it swung open, creaking on rusty hinges. It swung open—*on the face of madness* .

He screamed twice, short, frantic screams, as he tried to hide his eyes from the rotten, writhing horror behind the gate.

ALAN E. NOURSE

"Here!" he screamed. "It's here. You're at the right place. This is what you're looking for. Cut it out. Slice it away. Please, I can't stand it any longer."

His feet moved through the horrible gate, into the swarming, loathsome, horror-ridden madness that lay beyond. And he screamed again as he saw the bright flash. He felt the wrenching, sickening lurch that took him and threw him to the ground, down the long, twisting channels of darkness, as the pain struck through his head.

Suddenly there was another blinding flash, and he felt his muscles and his mind crumble into dust. He fell and quivered and lay helplessly, as his mind sifted and drained away into the porous earth beneath him.

*

When he opened his eyes, he saw Conroe's face. He was tense for a moment, every muscle going into spasm. Then suddenly he relaxed and blinked and stared up at Conroe's face, his eyes filled with wonder.

"I'm sorry, Jeff. I don't know the words to tell you how sorry." There were tears in Conroe's eyes, and Jeff watched them and felt a chill of wonder run down his spine. For Conroe was not using words at all and yet he *knew* what Conroe wanted to say.

Wordlessly he reached up, took the man's hand, pressed it briefly and let it fall on the blanket again. "There aren't those kinds of words," he murmured.

"And you feel all right?"

Jeff blinked, sudden wonder dawning in his eyes. "I—I—I'm alive!" He struggled to sit up, felt the twinge of pain shoot down his spine.

Schiml moved up to the bedside and gently eased him back into the softness of the bed. "Yes," he said happily, "you're alive. And you're well. And there's no irony in calling you a Mercy Man." His eyes gleamed in happy triumph. "You're a whole man, Jeff—the way you were intended to be—for the first time in your life."

The words came to him clearly, yet Jeff knew that not a single word had been audible in the room. "Just like my father," he murmured. "I just felt him, just knew what he was thinking."

Tears were running down Schiml's cheeks, and his face was so infinitely happy that he hardly seemed the same man. He raised a finger, silently pointed to the water glass on the table and looked at Jeff. Jeff turned his

113

eyes to the glass, and it rose half an inch from the table and hung there, glowing slightly in the dim light of the room. Then it gently set back on the stand.

"Control," Jeff said softly. "I have control."

"The power was chained down to something else," Schiml said softly. "You had the extra-sensory power, yes, but it was linked to something that would have prevented you from ever gaining control. A degenerative insanity, part and parcel of the extra-sensory power. You're not alone, Jeff. There are many hundreds like you, in greater or lesser degrees. Conroe is like you, to a very limited extent. And he's been seeking a way to separate the two, for years. That's why you're really a Mercy Man. We knew there were two centers, but we knew no way to separate them. We had to have you to guide us, Jeff. We had to find the center of insanity in your brain to cut it out and deliver you. That's what we've waited twenty years for. And you're free, now. It's gone. And now we have a technique we can use to free a thousand others like you."

Jeff stared at them wonderingly. Sunlight streamed in the window. Across the way, he could see the ward-towers of the Hoffman Medical Center, white and gleaming. He took a deep breath of the fresh air and turned again to the two men standing by the bedside.

"Then it was you who were hunting me," he murmured. "Strange, isn't it. It wasn't me hunting Conroe. It was my father, the ghost of my father still in my mind. The ghost of a madman—" His eyes narrowed and he stared at Schiml closely. "Then there were others who knew too. Blackie knew. She must have been the girl in the night club."

"She was. A little heavy make-up, a little light plastic, those made enough change to deceive you. But she never knew why. Hypnotics can be powerful and they can erase all memory." He paused, smiling at Jeff. "Blackie will be next. We need her so much in the work we have to do, almost as much as we need you. But you've freed Blackie too. She'll be happier than she's ever been since the cloak of bad luck began broadcasting from her mind ten years ago. She'll be happier by far."

*

Hours later, Jeff woke again in the still room. The men were gone and the shadows were lengthening in the room, and his mind was filled with many thoughts.

114

ALAN E. NOURSE

"You can go if you want," Paul Conroe had said before they left. "Or you can stay, as you see fit. If you go, we can't stop you. But we beg you to stay. We need you so very much."

There would be others staying, Jeff thought. The Nasty Frenchman would stay—sneering, laughing, hating—aiming at the big money that always lurked in the future, unaware completely of the errand of mercy he was running with his life. And Harpo would stay, and all the others....

And Blackie would stay too. Poor, helpless Blackie—beautiful Blackie, desperate Blackie. For her there was a new lease. And there was no way of telling the person she would be after the new lease was signed for her.

And Conroe would stay, delivered after all these years of the burden he carried.

Wearily, yet happily, Jeff stared at the ceiling. He breathed deeply of the quiet air, his mind filled with a maze of wondering thoughts. He knew that thinking now was useless, that there really wasn't any issue any more.

He knew, as he closed his eyes again, that Jeff Meyer would stay too.